BOFFIN BOY
AND THE
FOREST OF THE NINJA

By David Orme

Illustrated by Peter Richardson

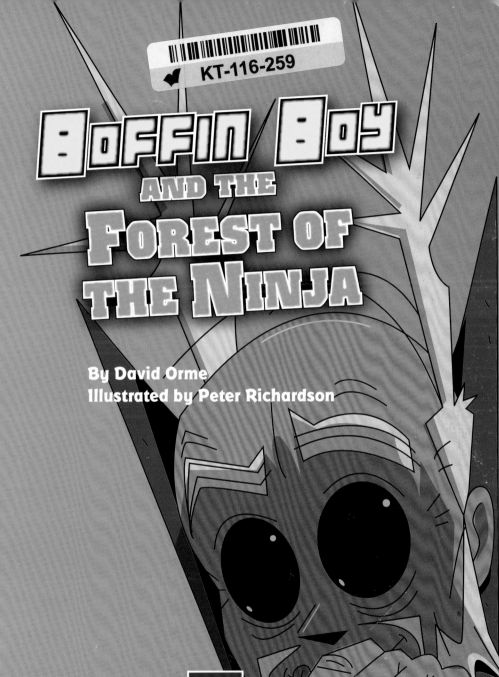

Ransom

COLLECT THE SET!

Boffin Boy and the Invaders from Space
978 184167 613 5

Boffin Boy and the Wizard of Edo
978 184167 614 2

Boffin Boy and the Monsters from the Deep
978 184167 615 9

Boffin Boy and the Red Wolf
978 184167 616 6

Boffin Boy and the Lost City
978 184167 617 3

Boffin Boy and the Time Warriors
978 184167 622 7

Boffin Boy and the Ice Caves of Pluto
978 184167 626 5

Boffin Boy and the Quest for Wisdom
978 184167 628 9

Boffin Boy and the Deadly Swarm
978 184167 625 8

Boffin Boy and the Rock Men
978 184167 624 1

Boffin Boy and the Temples of Mars
978 184167 623 4

Boffin Boy and the Forest of the Ninja
978 184167 627

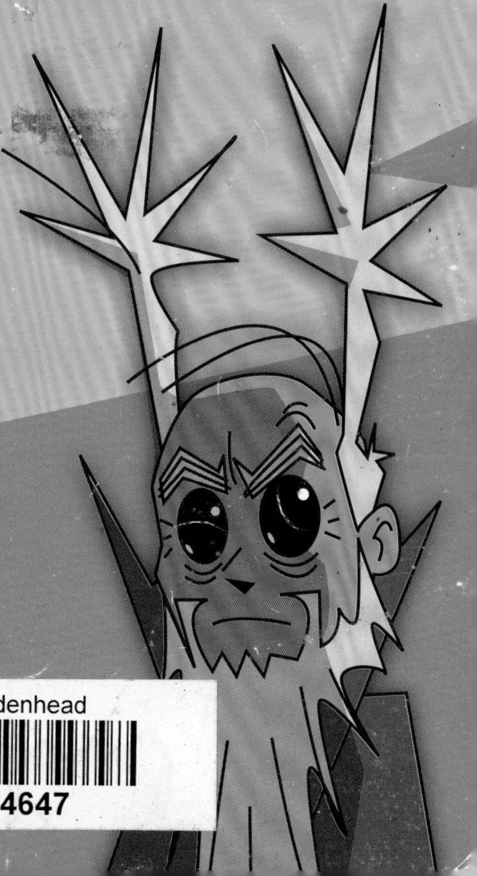

Boffin Boy and the Forest of the Ninja
by David Orme

Illustrated by Peter Richardson

Published by Ransom Publishing Ltd.
Radley House, 8 St. Cross Road, Winchester, Hants. SO23 9HX
www.ransom.co.uk

ISBN   978 184167 627 2
First published in 2007
Reprinted 2008, 2009, 2010
Copyright © 2007 Ransom Publishing Ltd.

Illustrations copyright © 2007 Peter Richardson

A CIP catalogue record of this book is available from the British
Library.

Design & layout: *www.macwiz.co.uk*

Find out more about Boffin Boy at *www.ransom.co.uk*.

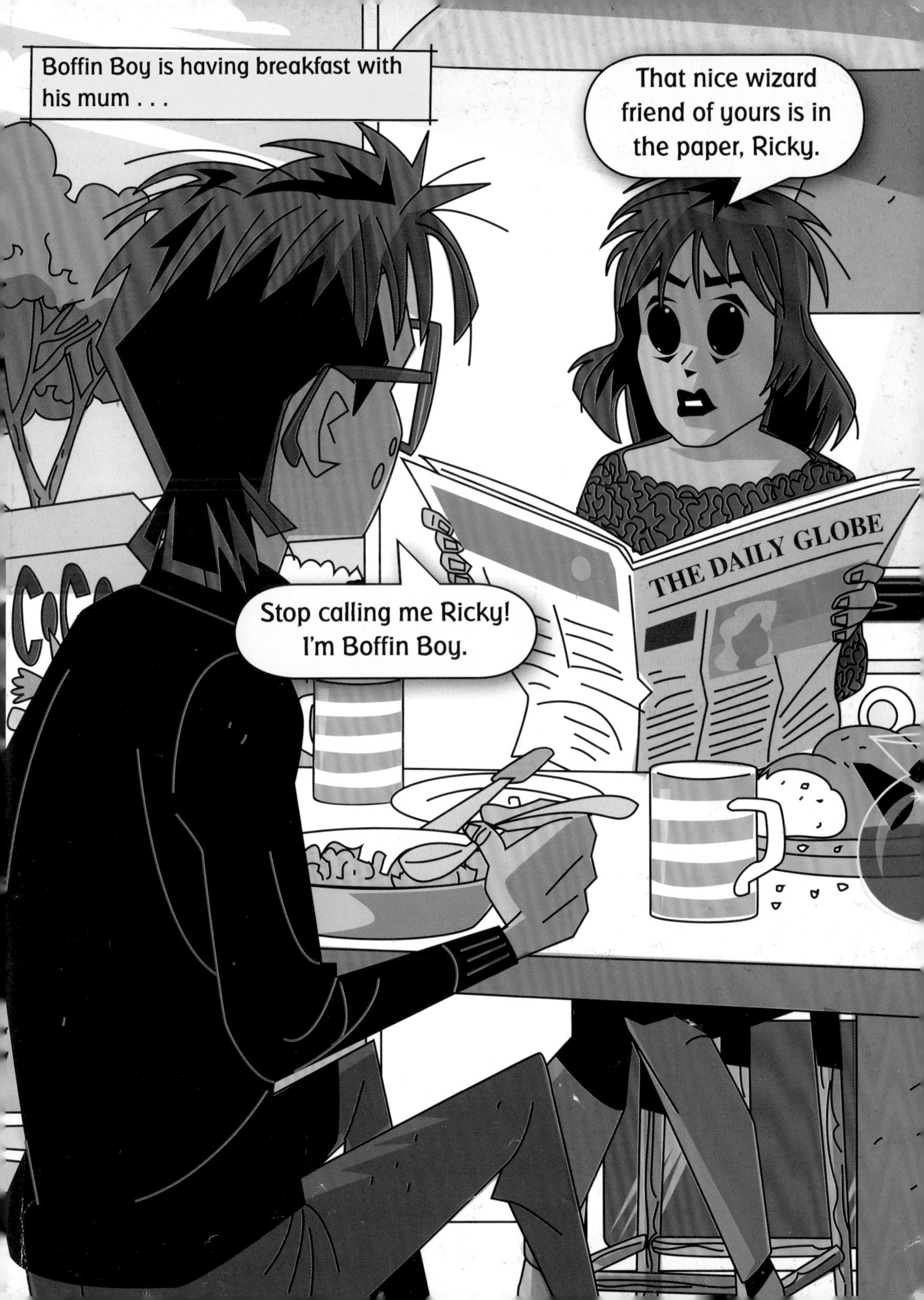

Boffin Boy is having breakfast with his mum . . .
That nice wizard friend of yours is in the paper, Ricky.
THE DAILY GLOBE
Stop calling me Ricky! I'm Boffin Boy.

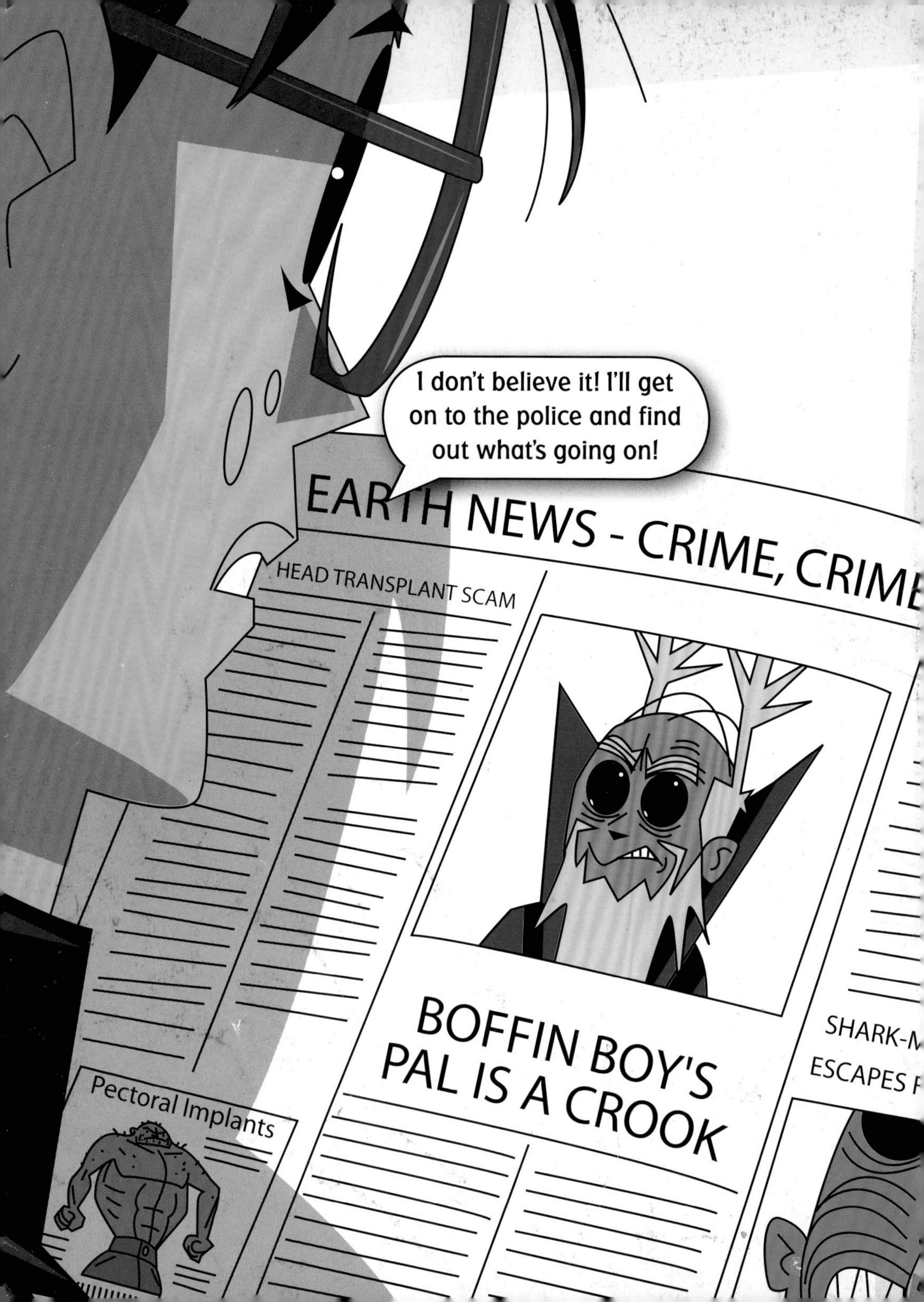
I don't believe it! I'll get on to the police and find out what's going on!
EARTH NEWS - CRIME, CRIME
HEAD TRANSPLANT SCAM
BOFFIN BOY'S PAL IS A CROOK
SHARK-M
ESCAPES F
Pectoral Implants

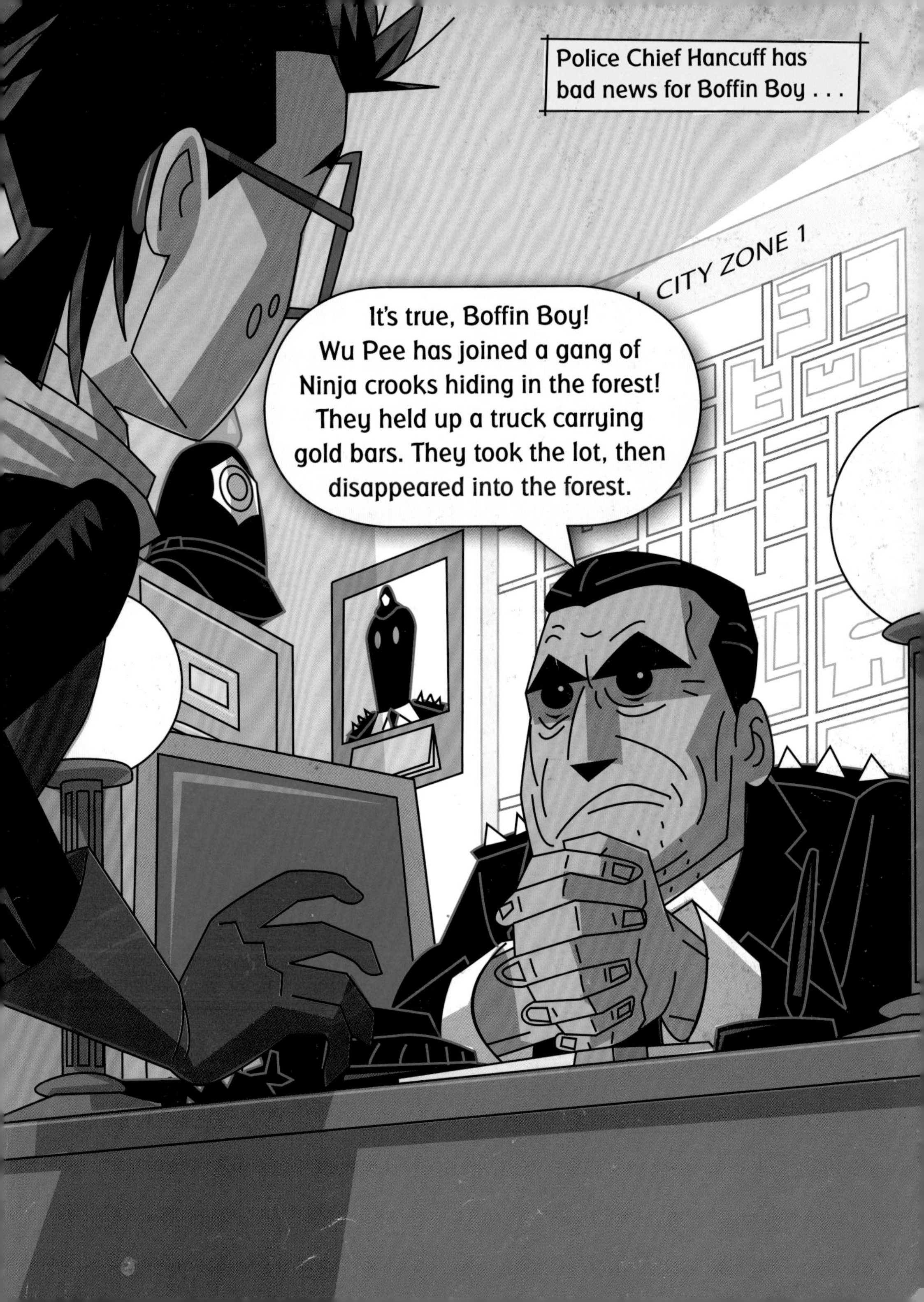

Police Chief Hancuff has bad news for Boffin Boy . . .
It's true, Boffin Boy! Wu Pee has joined a gang of Ninja crooks hiding in the forest! They held up a truck carrying gold bars. They took the lot, then disappeared into the forest.
CITY ZONE 1

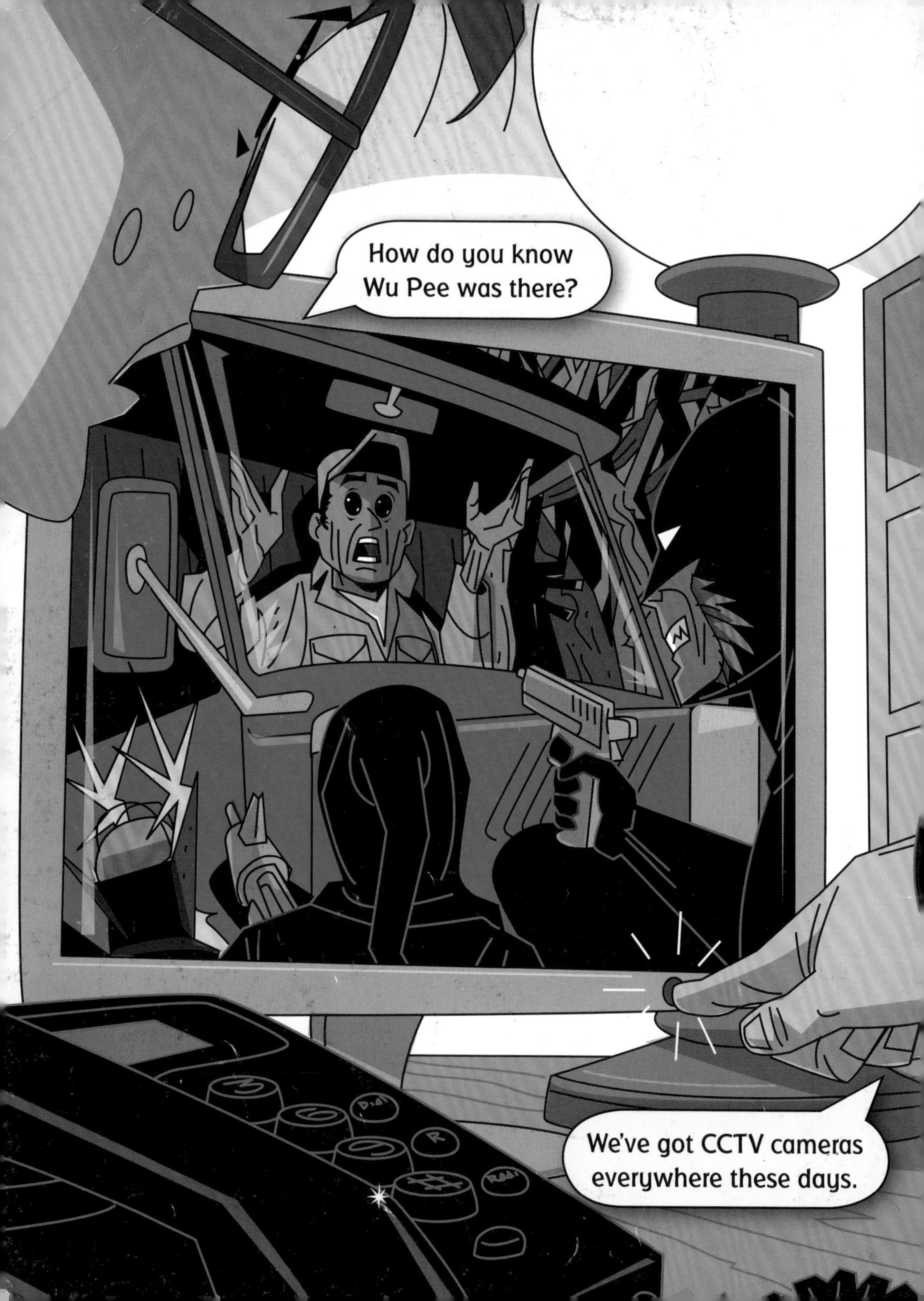
How do you know Wu Pee was there?
We've got CCTV cameras everywhere these days.

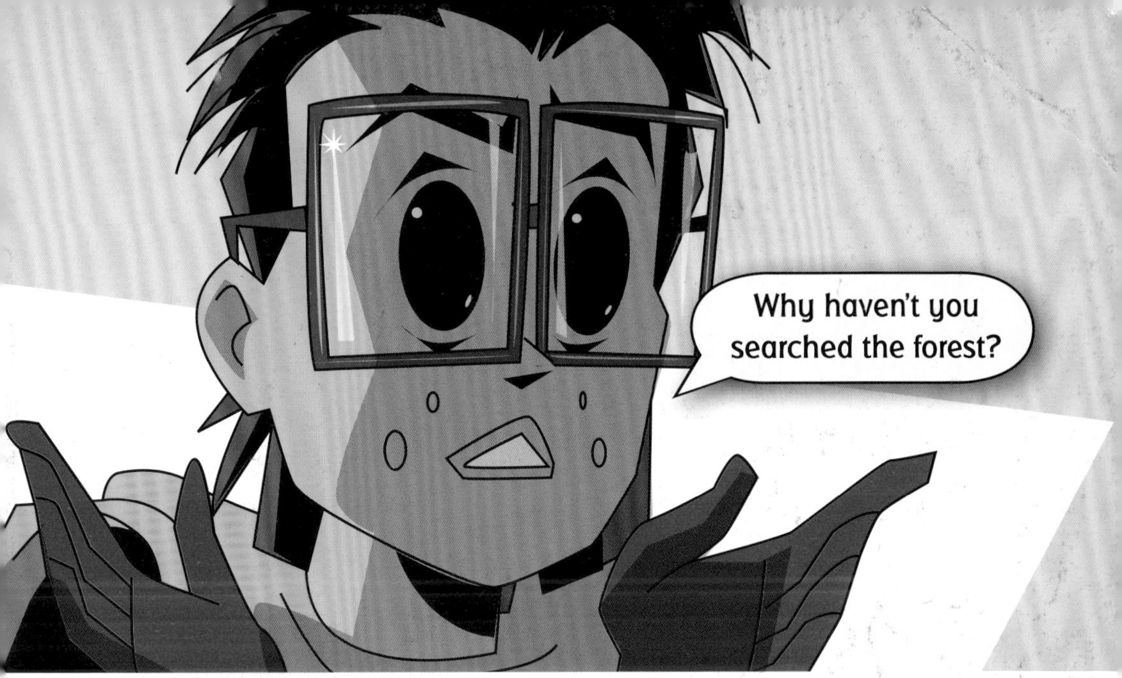
Why haven't you searched the forest?

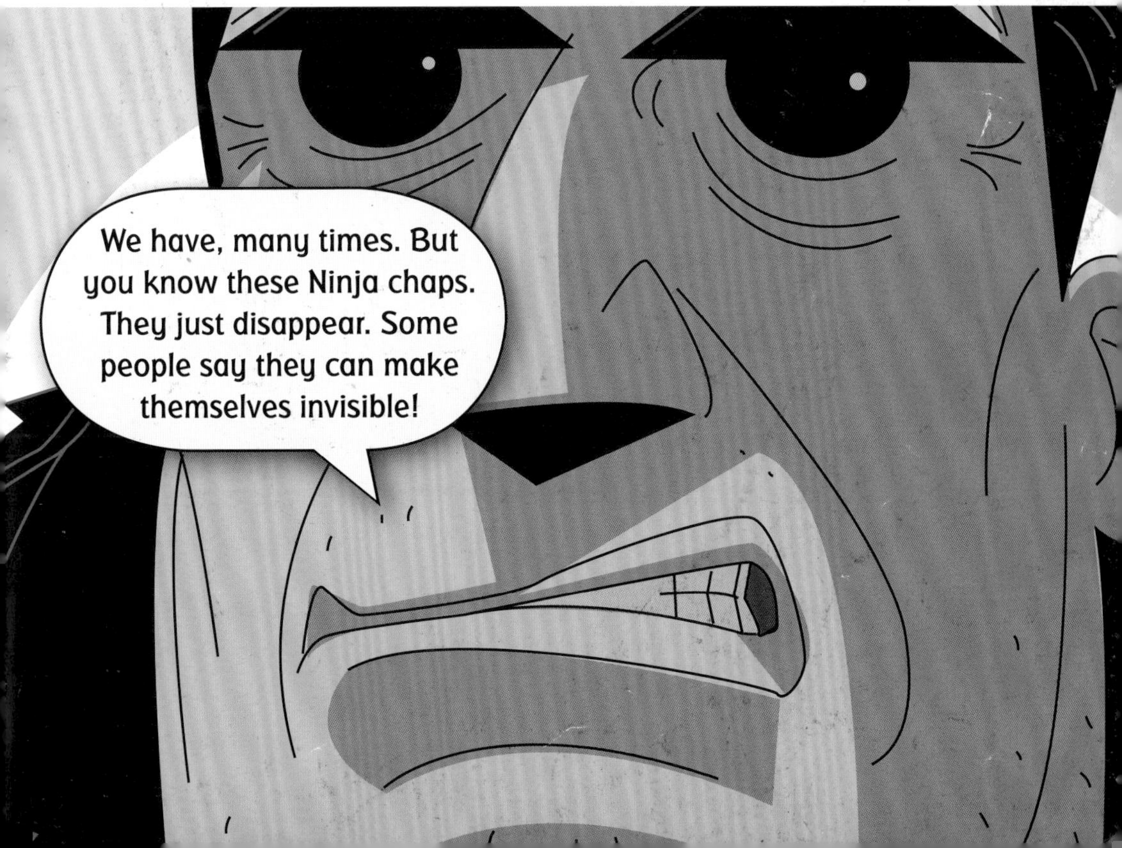
We have, many times. But you know these Ninja chaps. They just disappear. Some people say they can make themselves invisible!

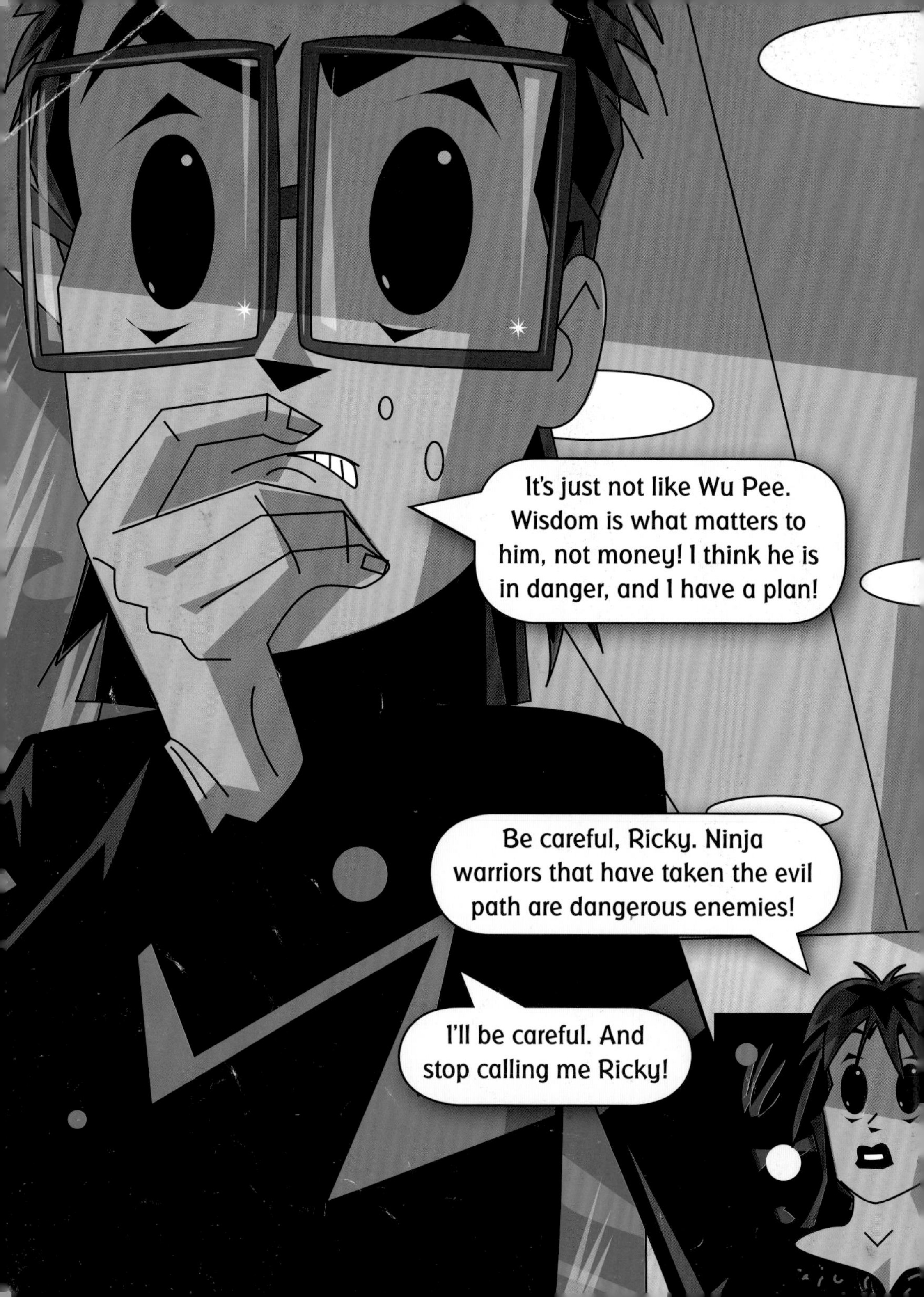
It's just not like Wu Pee. Wisdom is what matters to him, not money! I think he is in danger, and I have a plan!
Be careful, Ricky. Ninja warriors that have taken the evil path are dangerous enemies!
I'll be careful. And stop calling me Ricky!

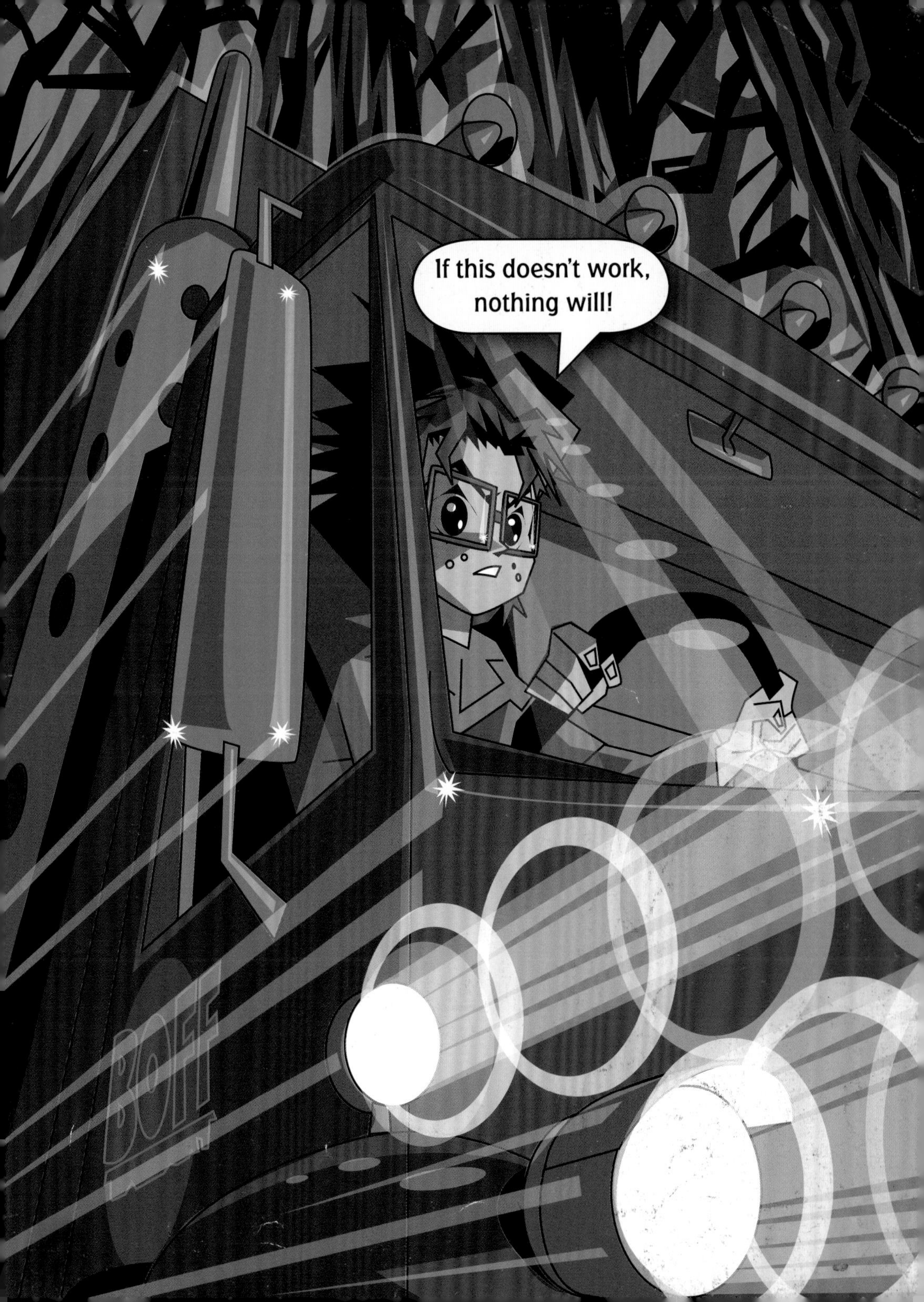
If this doesn't work, nothing will!
BOFF

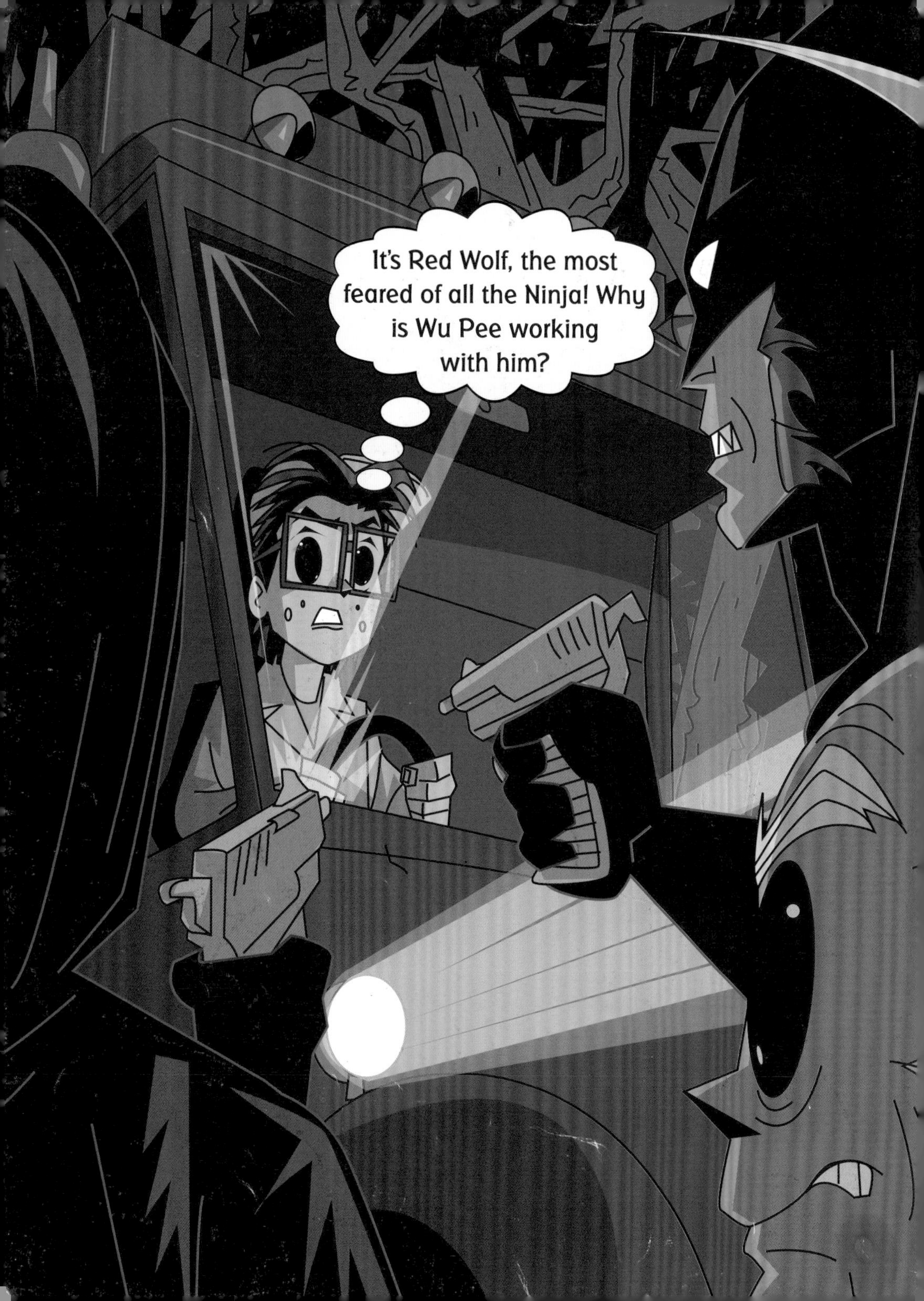
It's Red Wolf, the most feared of all the Ninja! Why is Wu Pee working with him?

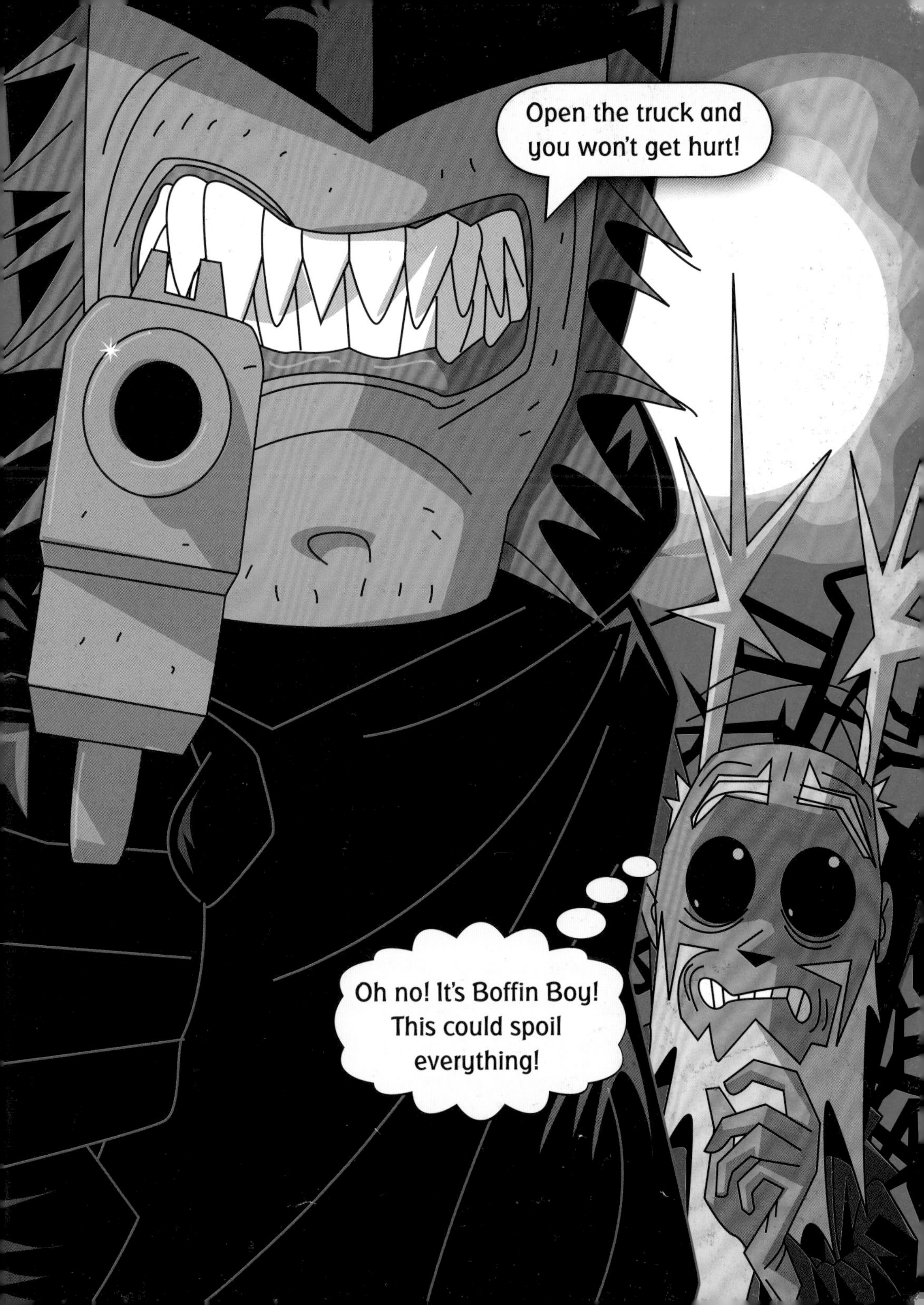
Open the truck and you won't get hurt!
Oh no! It's Boffin Boy! This could spoil everything!

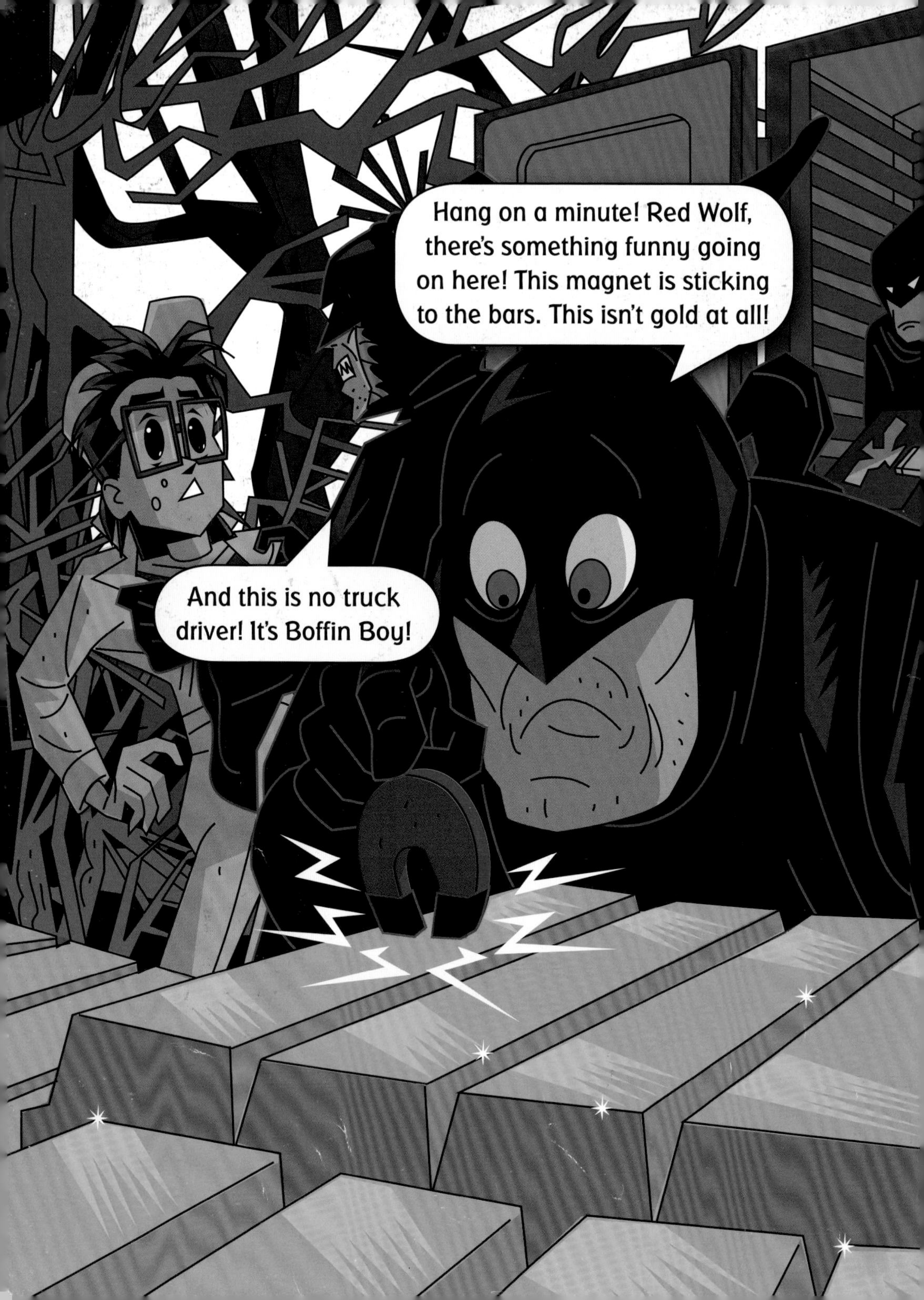
Hang on a minute! Red Wolf, there's something funny going on here! This magnet is sticking to the bars. This isn't gold at all!
And this is no truck driver! It's Boffin Boy!

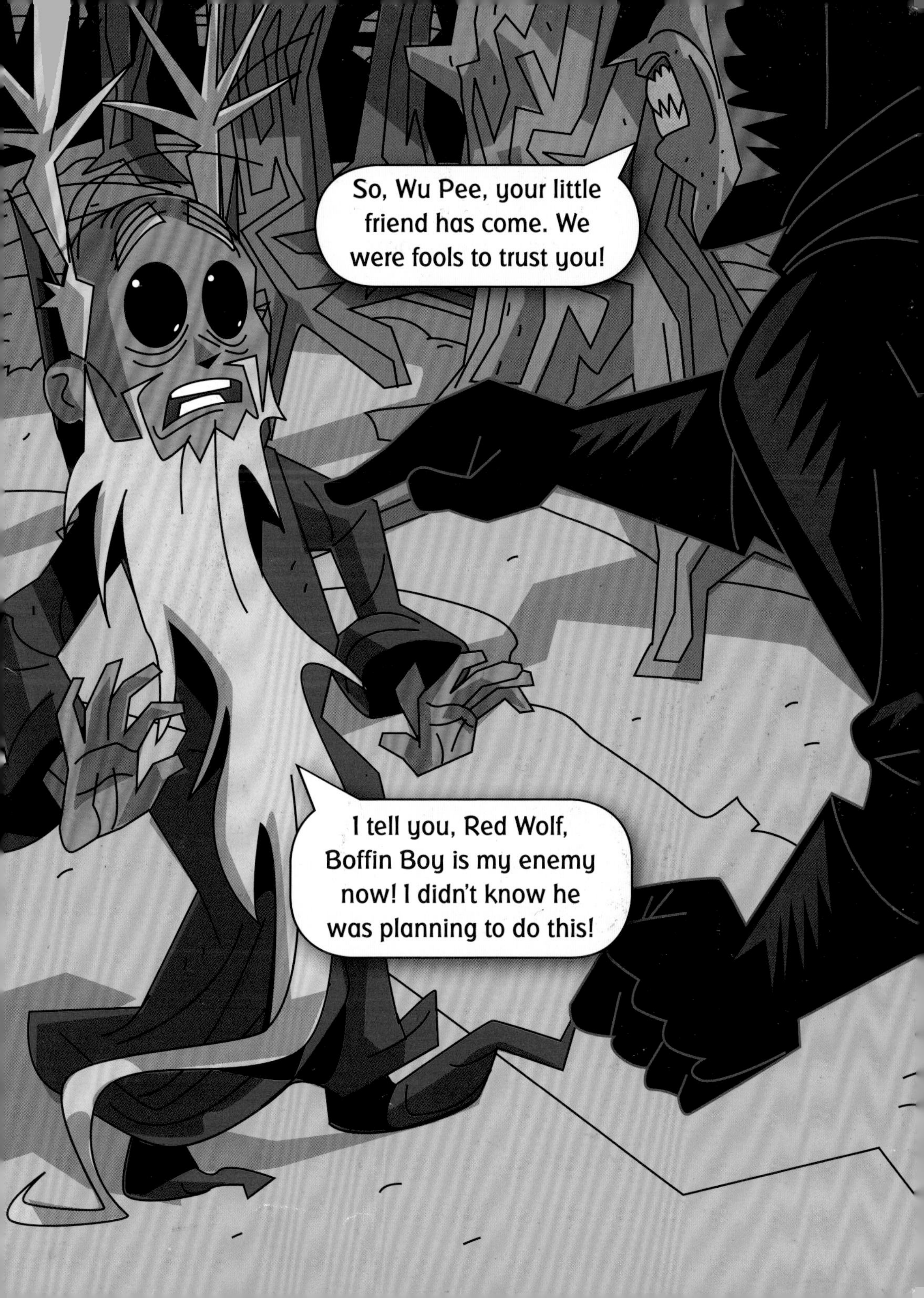
So, Wu Pee, your little friend has come. We were fools to trust you!
I tell you, Red Wolf, Boffin Boy is my enemy now! I didn't know he was planning to do this!

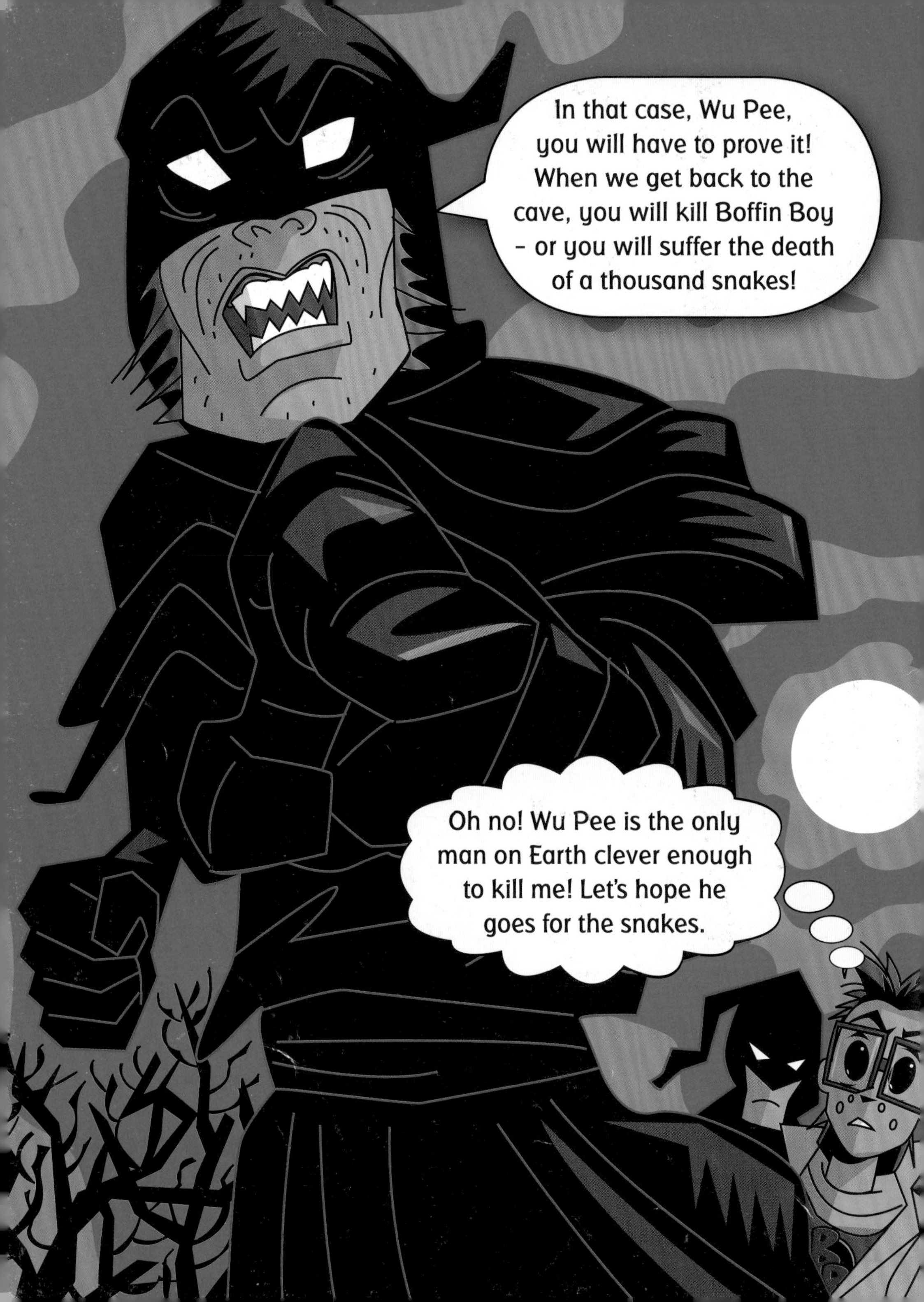
In that case, Wu Pee, you will have to prove it! When we get back to the cave, you will kill Boffin Boy - or you will suffer the death of a thousand snakes!
Oh no! Wu Pee is the only man on Earth clever enough to kill me! Let's hope he goes for the snakes.

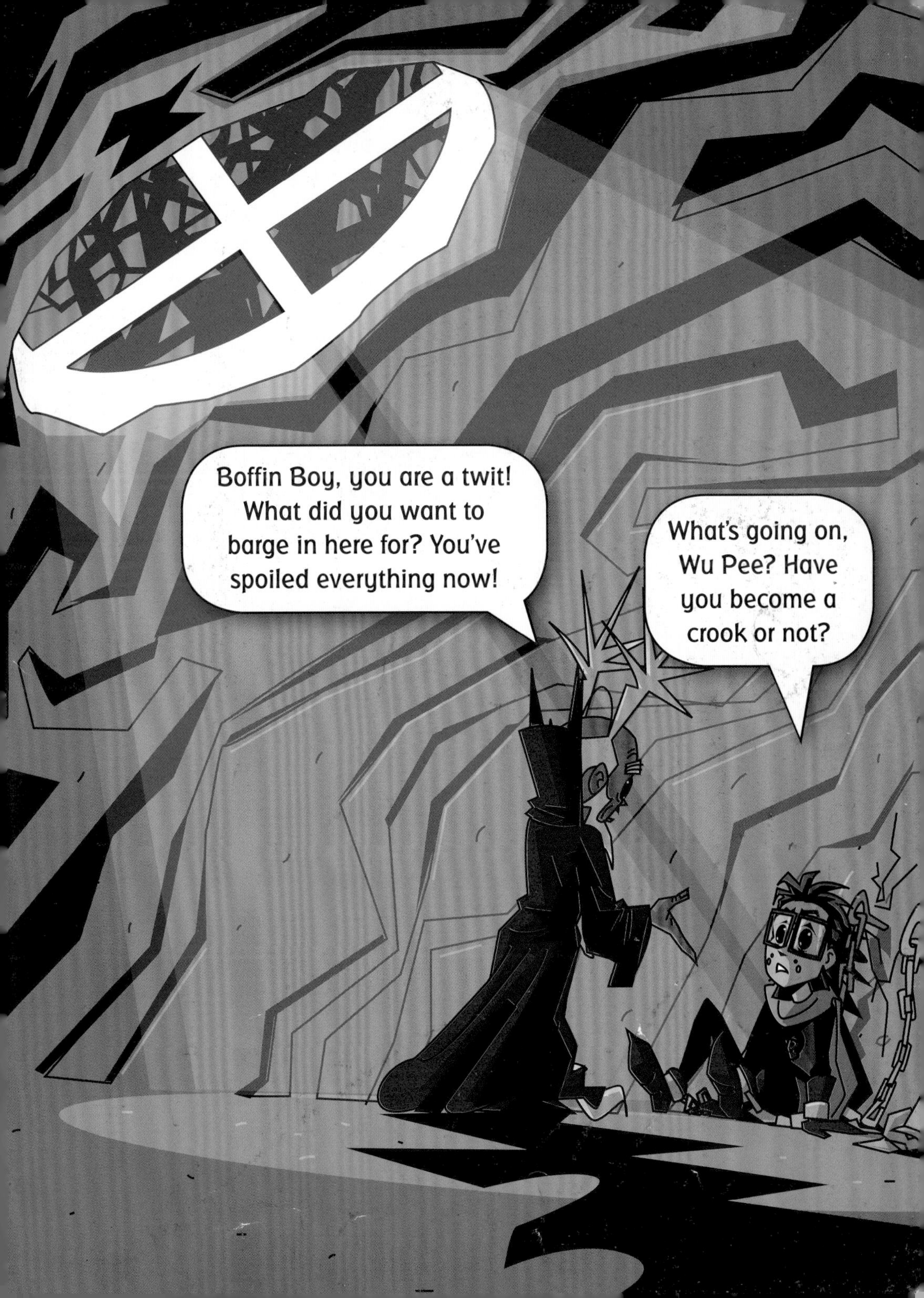
Boffin Boy, you are a twit! What did you want to barge in here for? You've spoiled everything now!
What's going on, Wu Pee? Have you become a crook or not?

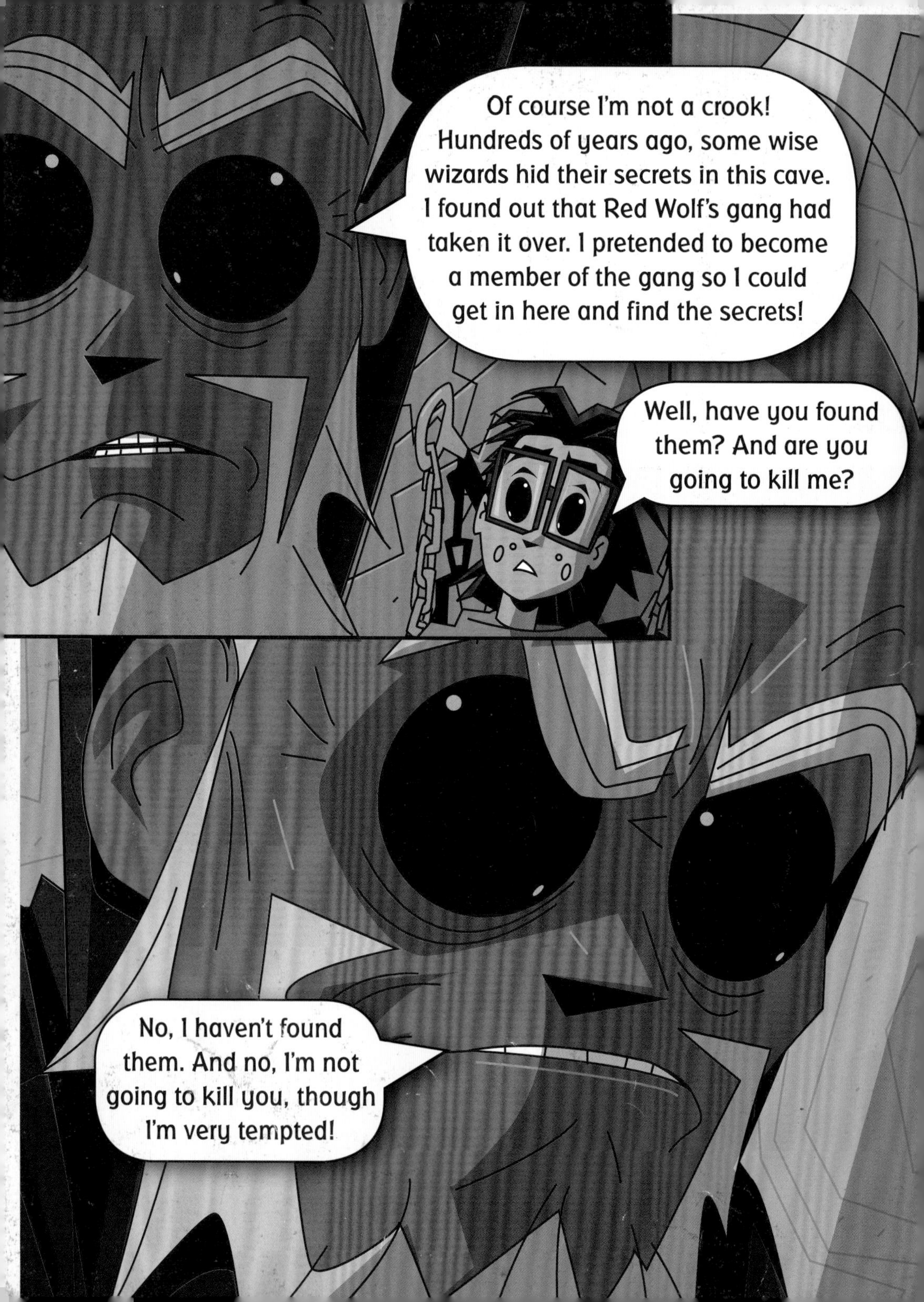
Of course I'm not a crook! Hundreds of years ago, some wise wizards hid their secrets in this cave. I found out that Red Wolf's gang had taken it over. I pretended to become a member of the gang so I could get in here and find the secrets!
Well, have you found them? And are you going to kill me?
No, I haven't found them. And no, I'm not going to kill you, though I'm very tempted!

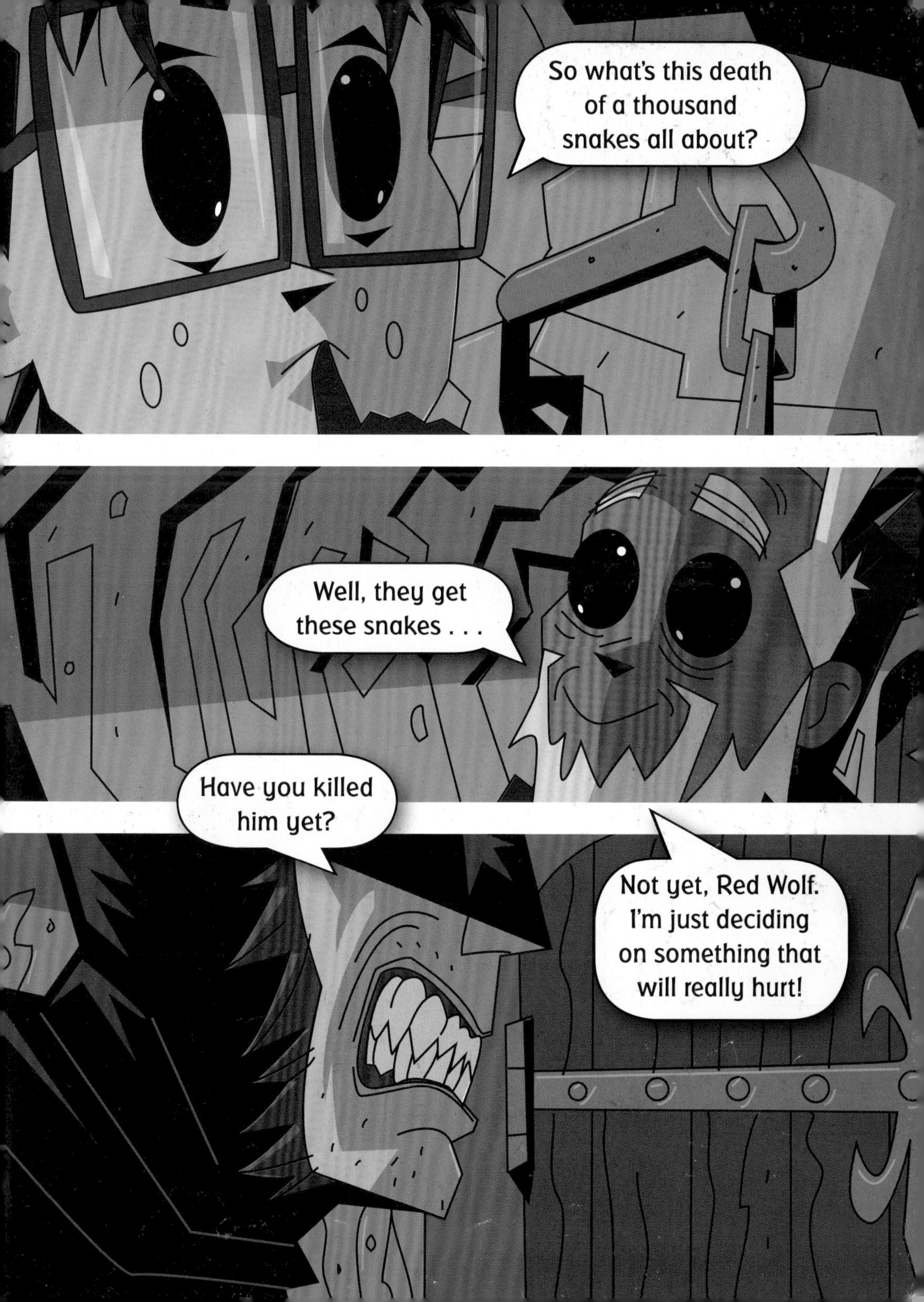
So what's this death of a thousand snakes all about?
Well, they get these snakes . . .
Have you killed him yet?
Not yet, Red Wolf. I'm just deciding on something that will really hurt!

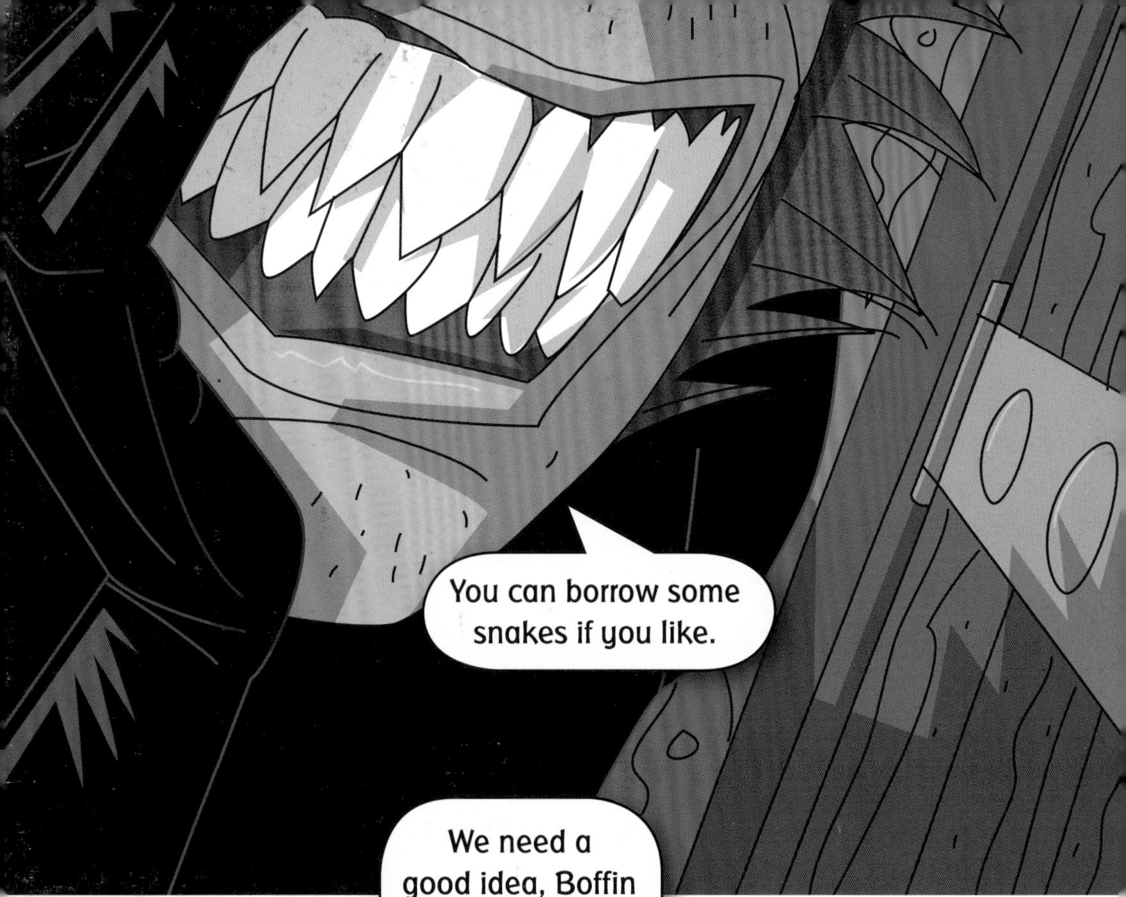
You can borrow some snakes if you like.

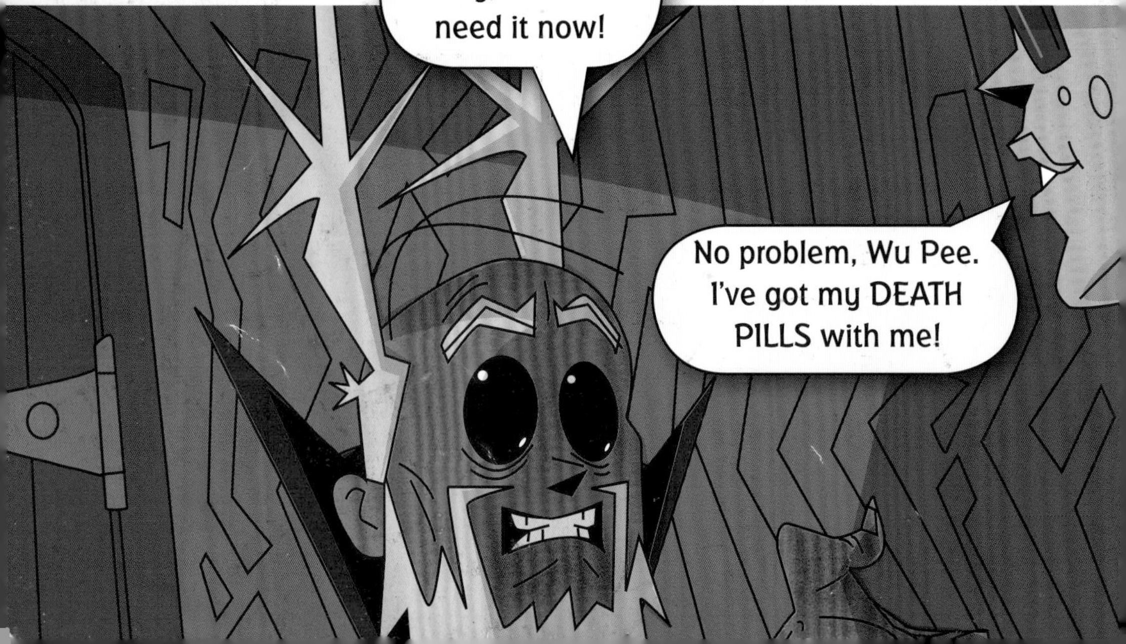
We need a good idea, Boffin Boy, and we need it now!
No problem, Wu Pee. I've got my DEATH PILLS with me!

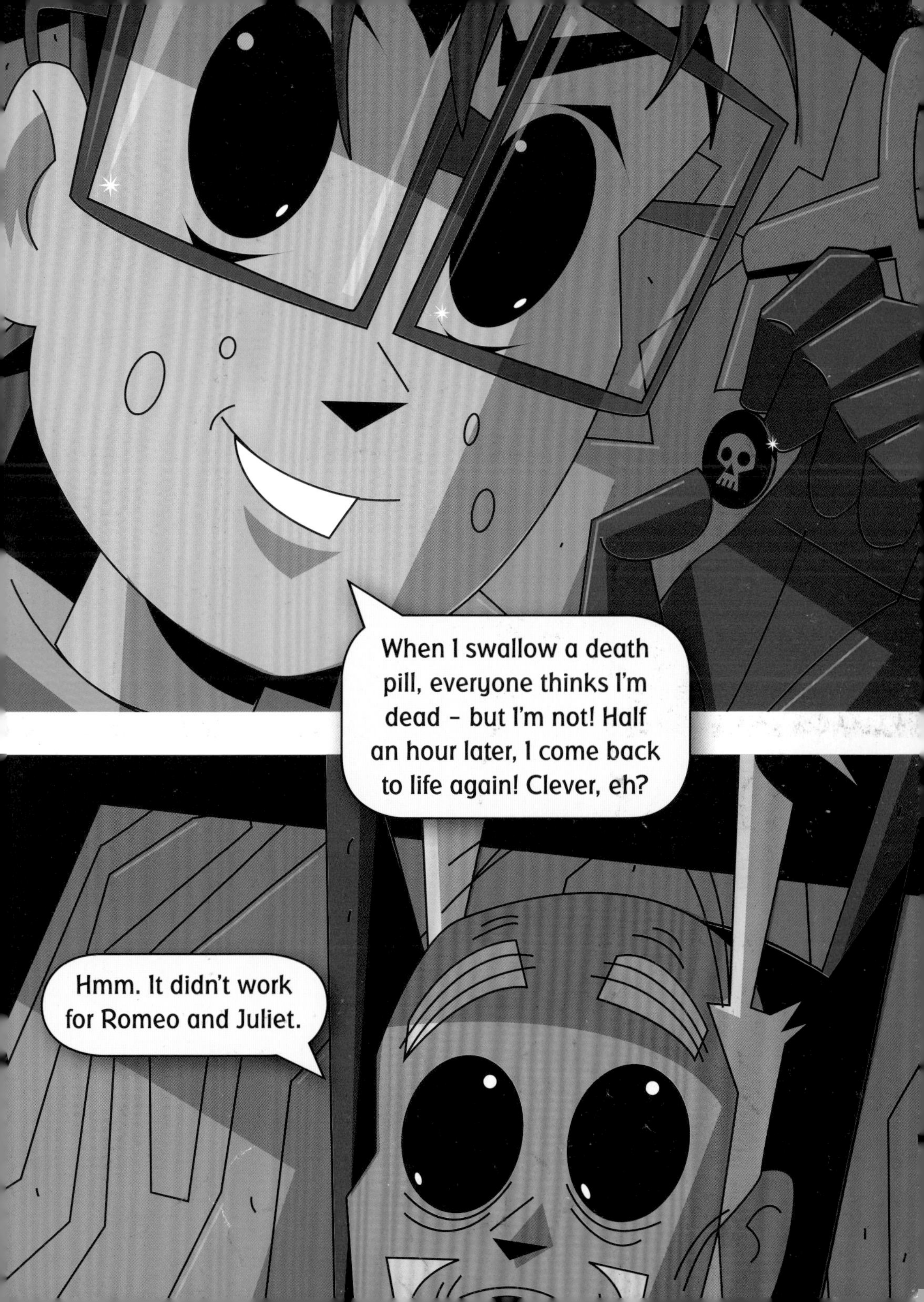
When I swallow a death pill, everyone thinks I'm dead – but I'm not! Half an hour later, I come back to life again! Clever, eh?
Hmm. It didn't work for Romeo and Juliet.

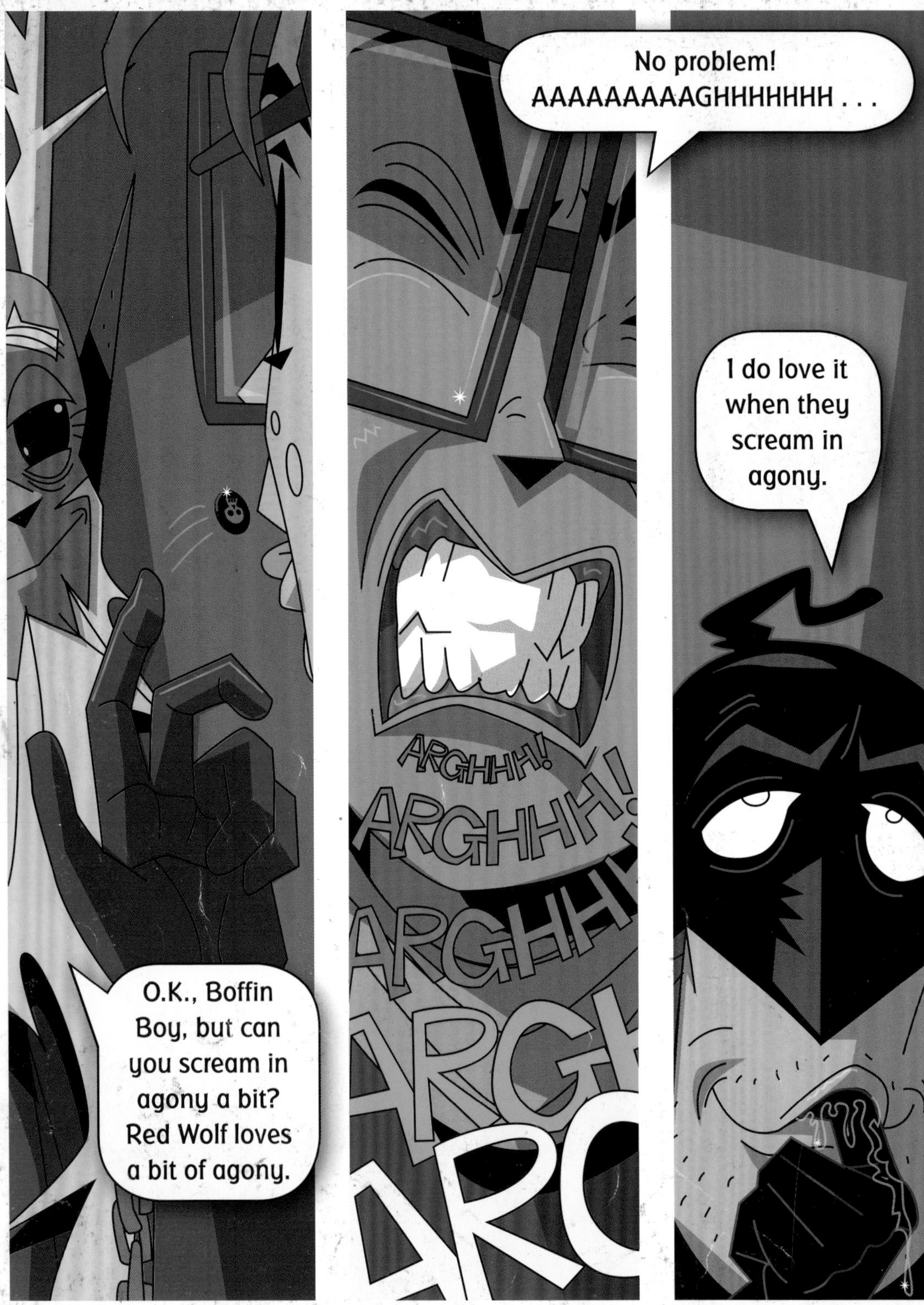
O.K., Boffin Boy, but can you scream in agony a bit? Red Wolf loves a bit of agony.
No problem! AAAAAAAAAGHHHHHHH . . .
ARGHHH!
ARGHHH!
I do love it when they scream in agony.

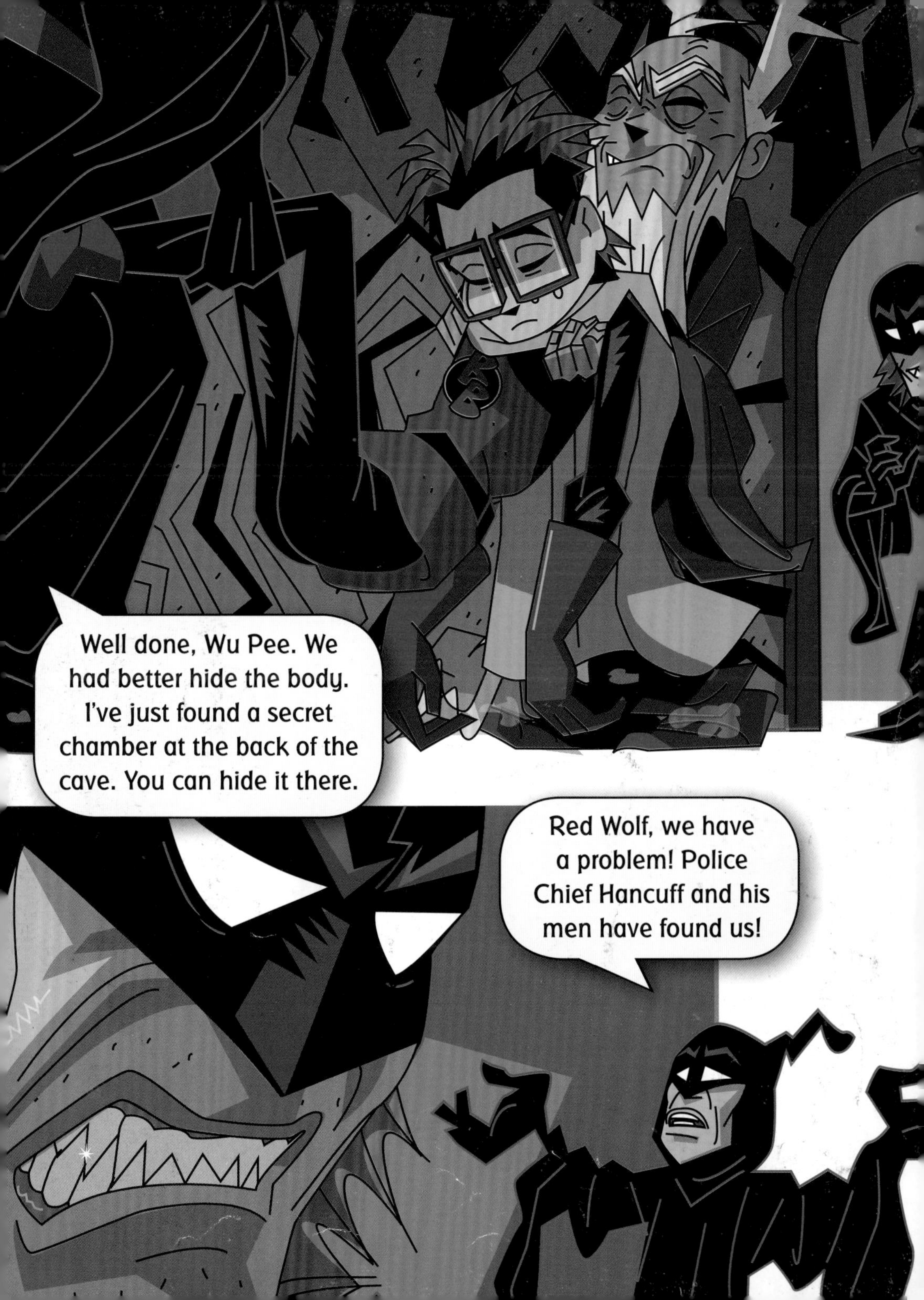
Well done, Wu Pee. We had better hide the body. I've just found a secret chamber at the back of the cave. You can hide it there.
Red Wolf, we have a problem! Police Chief Hancuff and his men have found us!

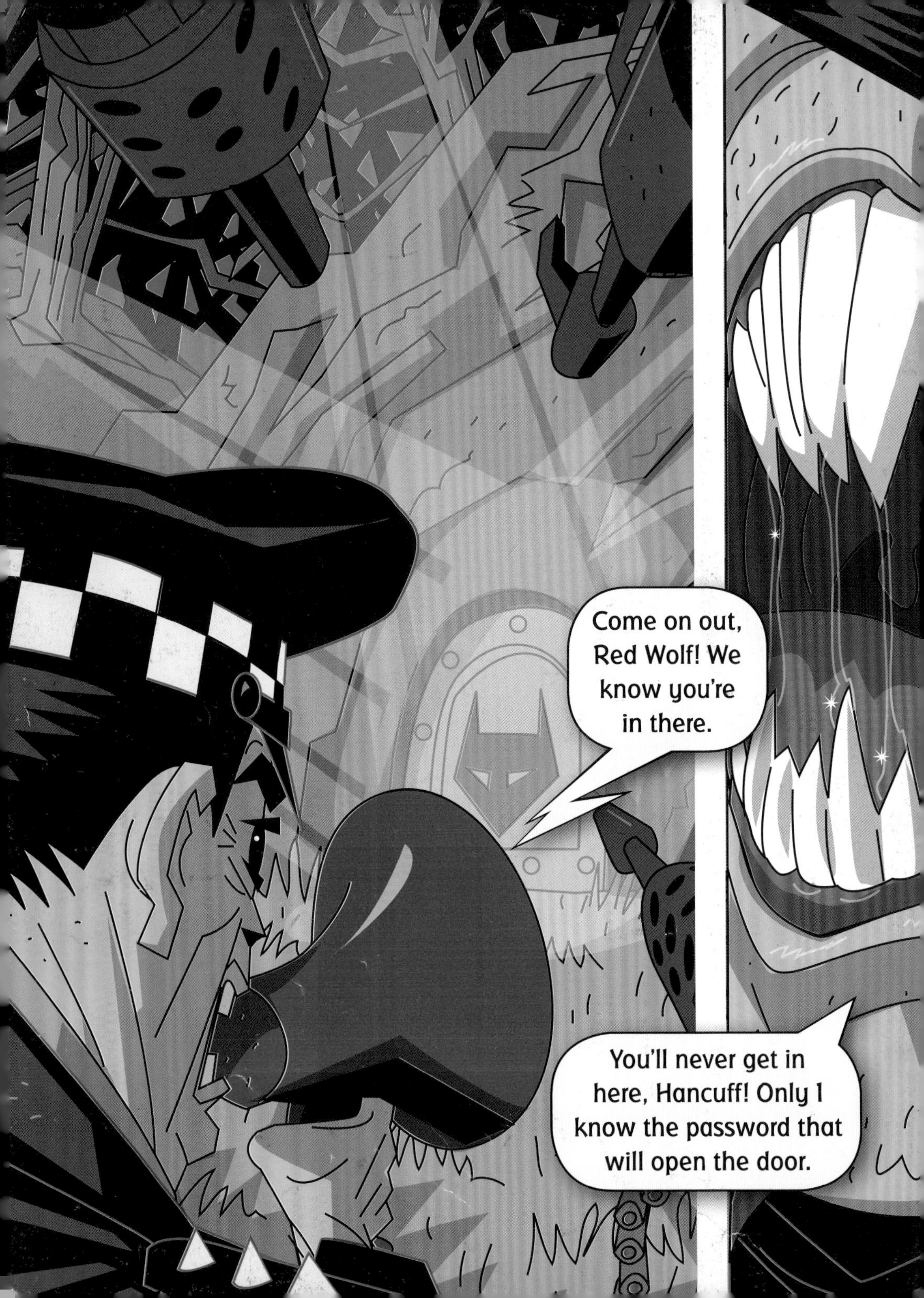
Come on out, Red Wolf! We know you're in there.
You'll never get in here, Hancuff! Only I know the password that will open the door.

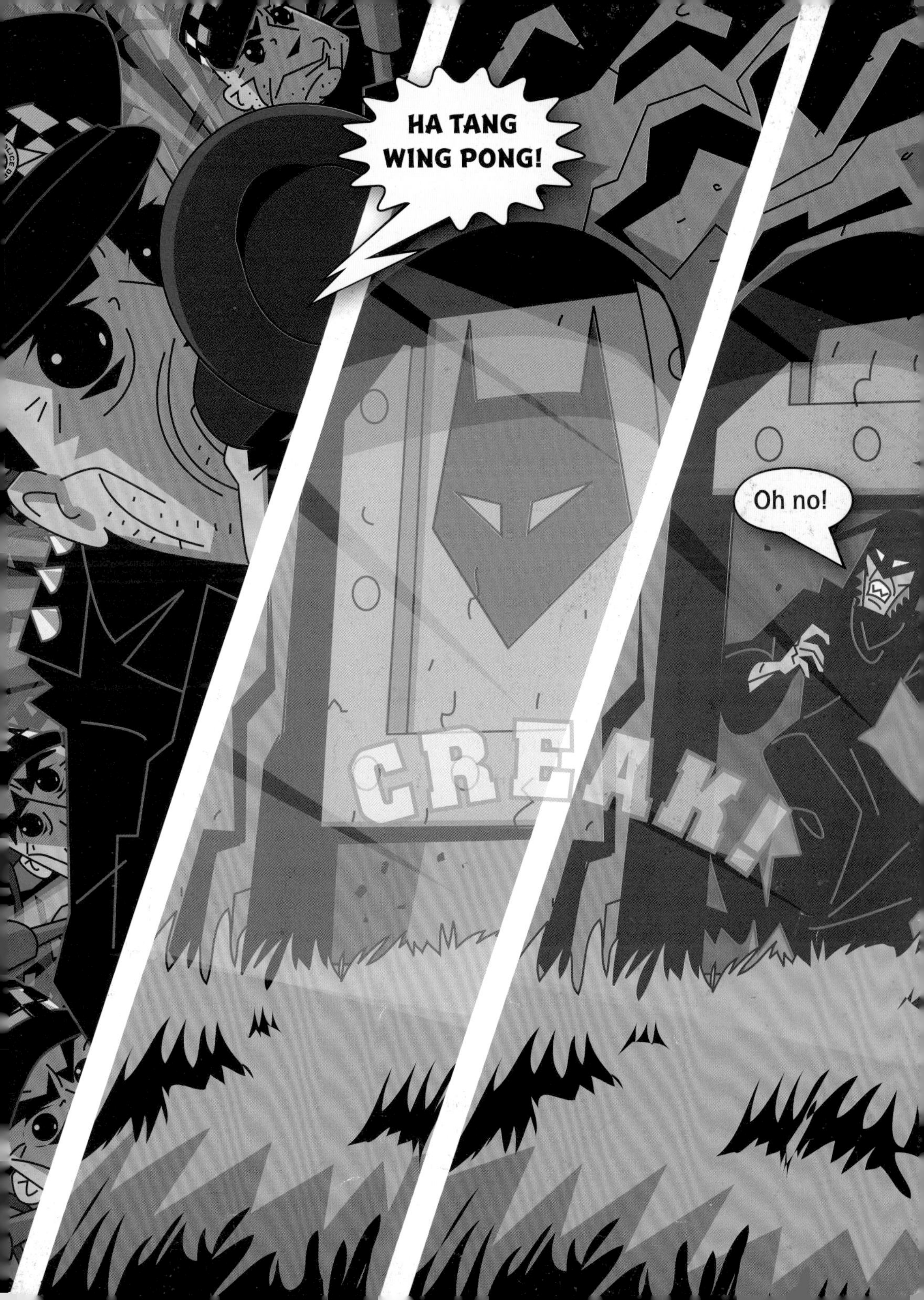
HA TANG WING PONG!
CREAK!
Oh no!

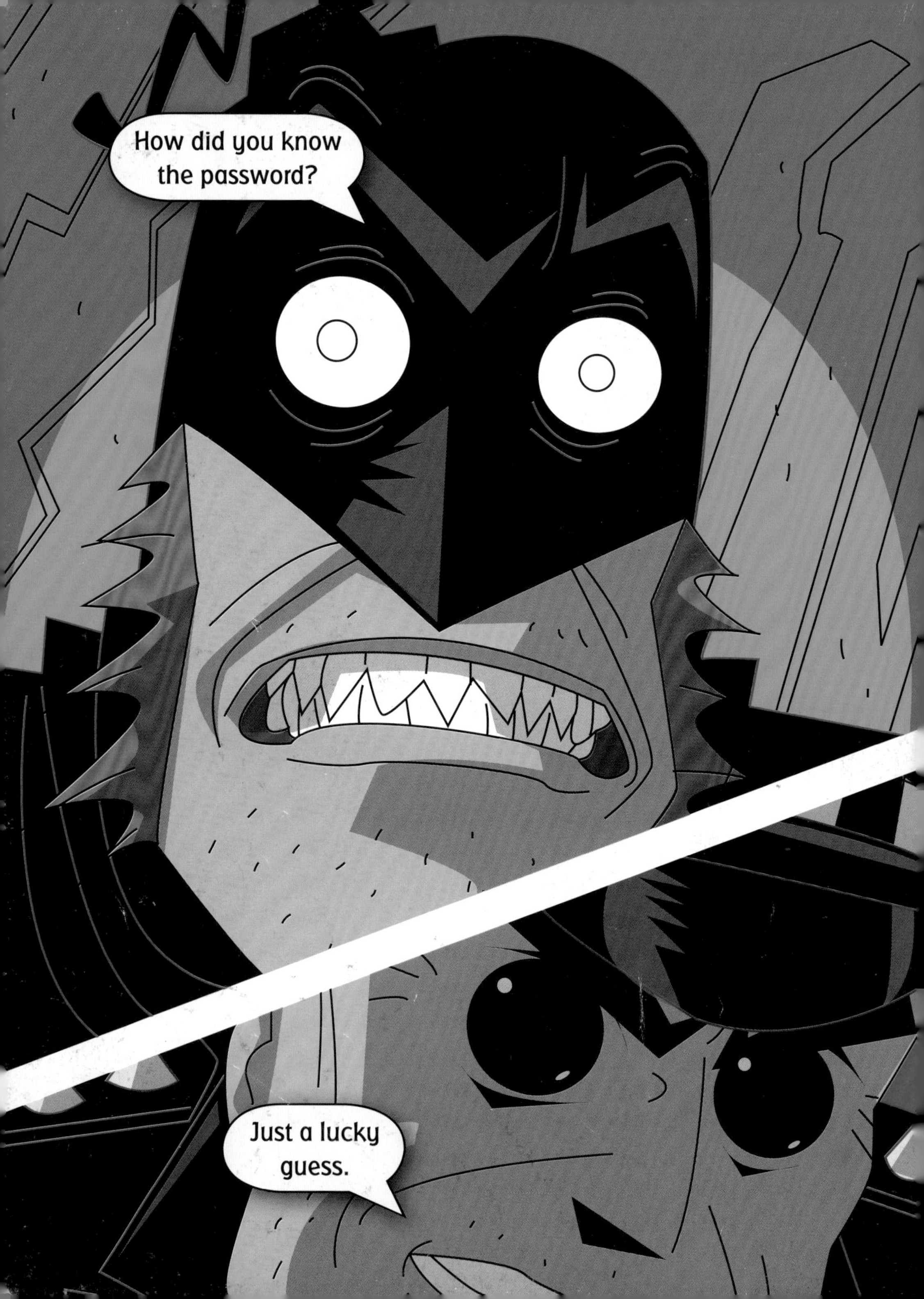
How did you know the password?
Just a lucky guess.

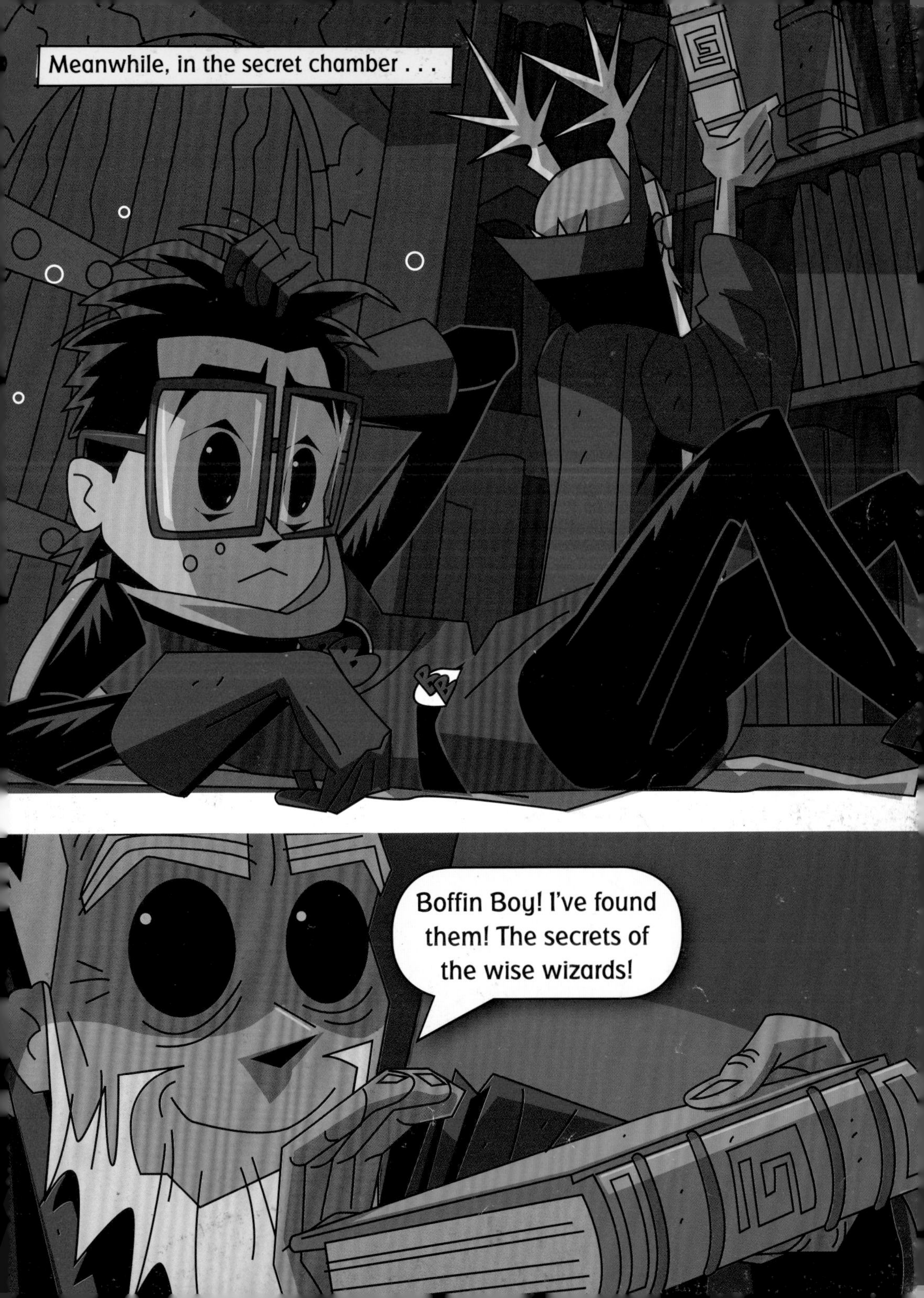
Meanwhile, in the secret chamber . . .
Boffin Boy! I've found them! The secrets of the wise wizards!

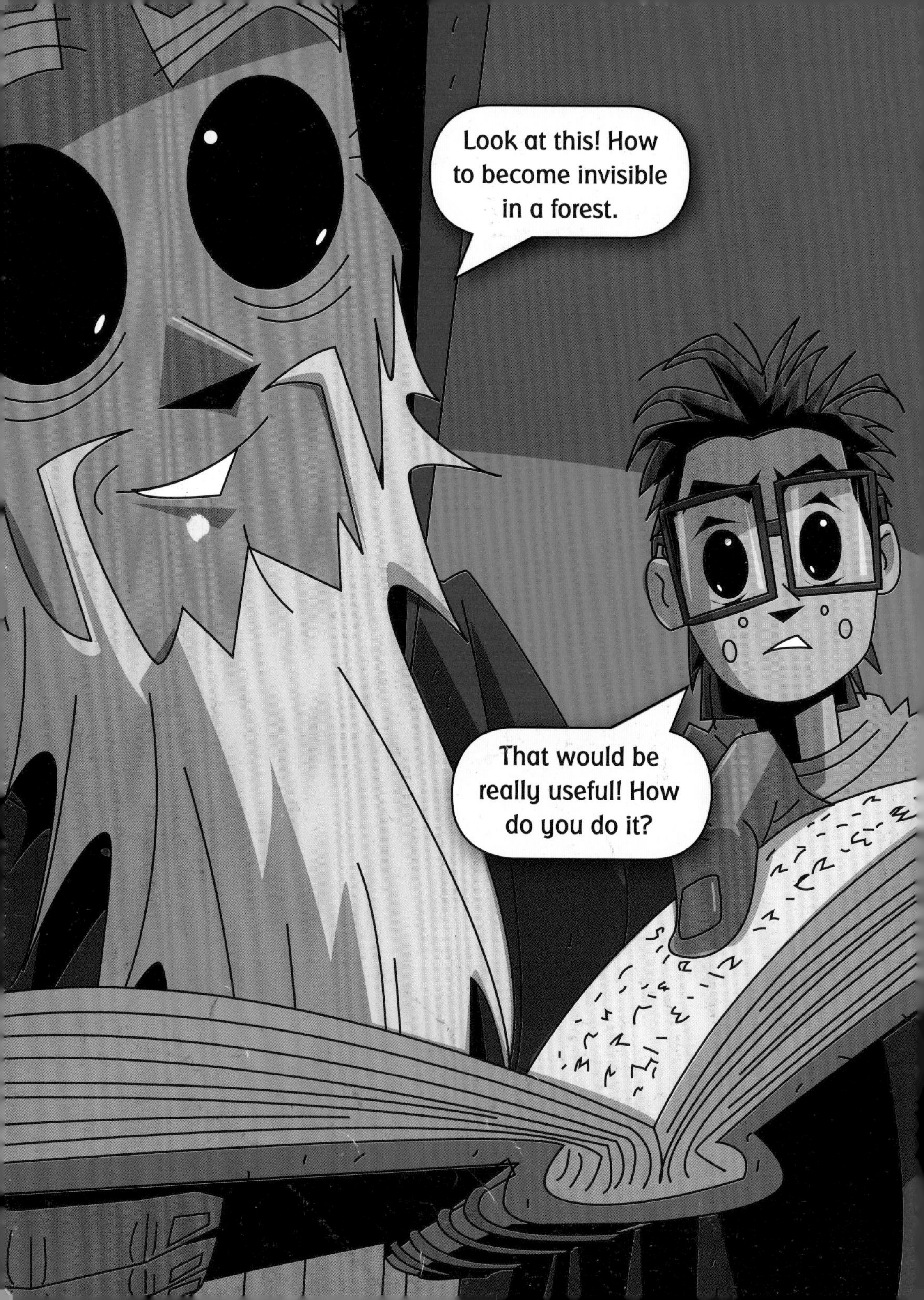
Look at this! How to become invisible in a forest.
That would be really useful! How do you do it?

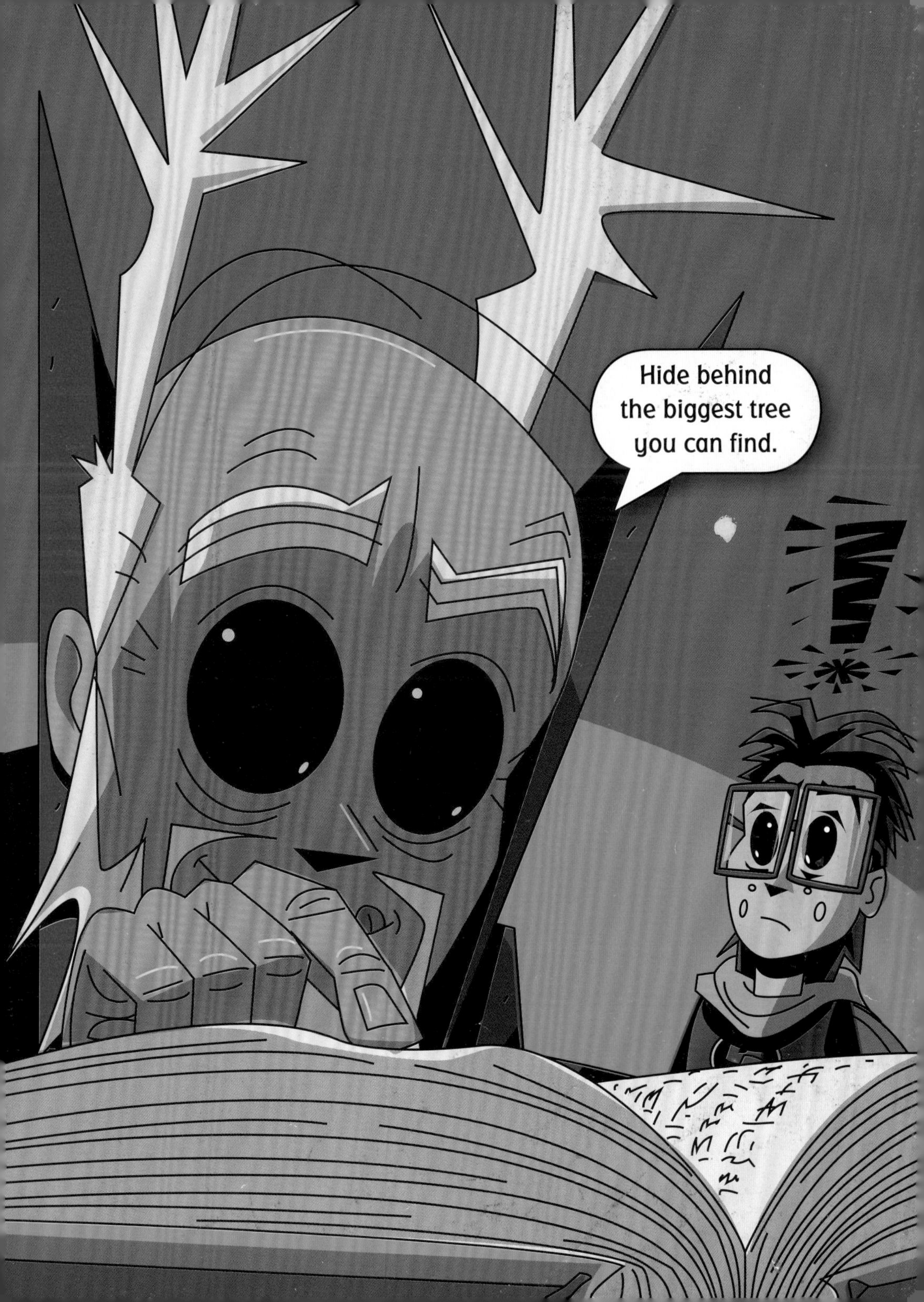
Hide behind the biggest tree you can find.

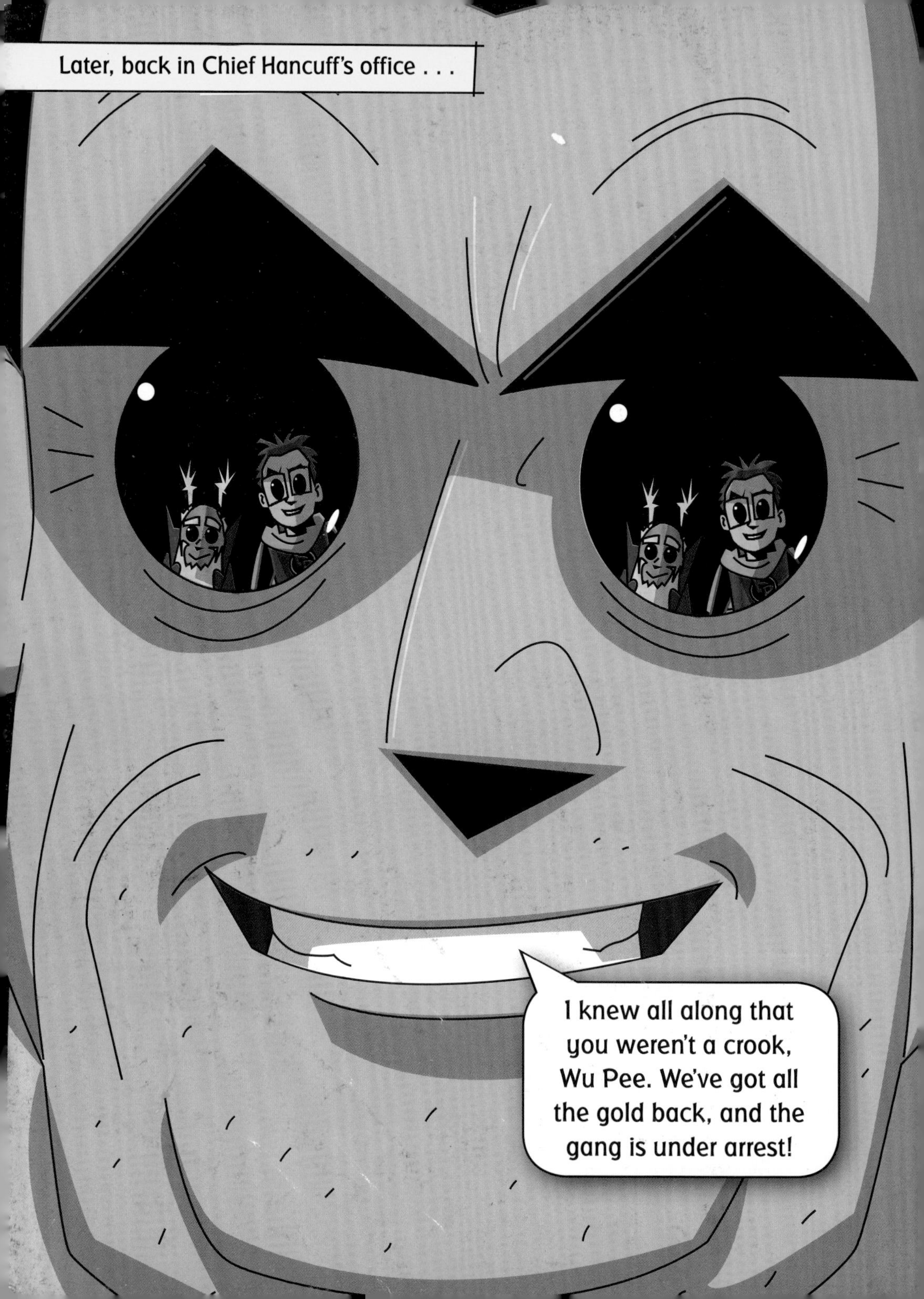
Later, back in Chief Hancuff's office . . .
I knew all along that you weren't a crook, Wu Pee. We've got all the gold back, and the gang is under arrest!

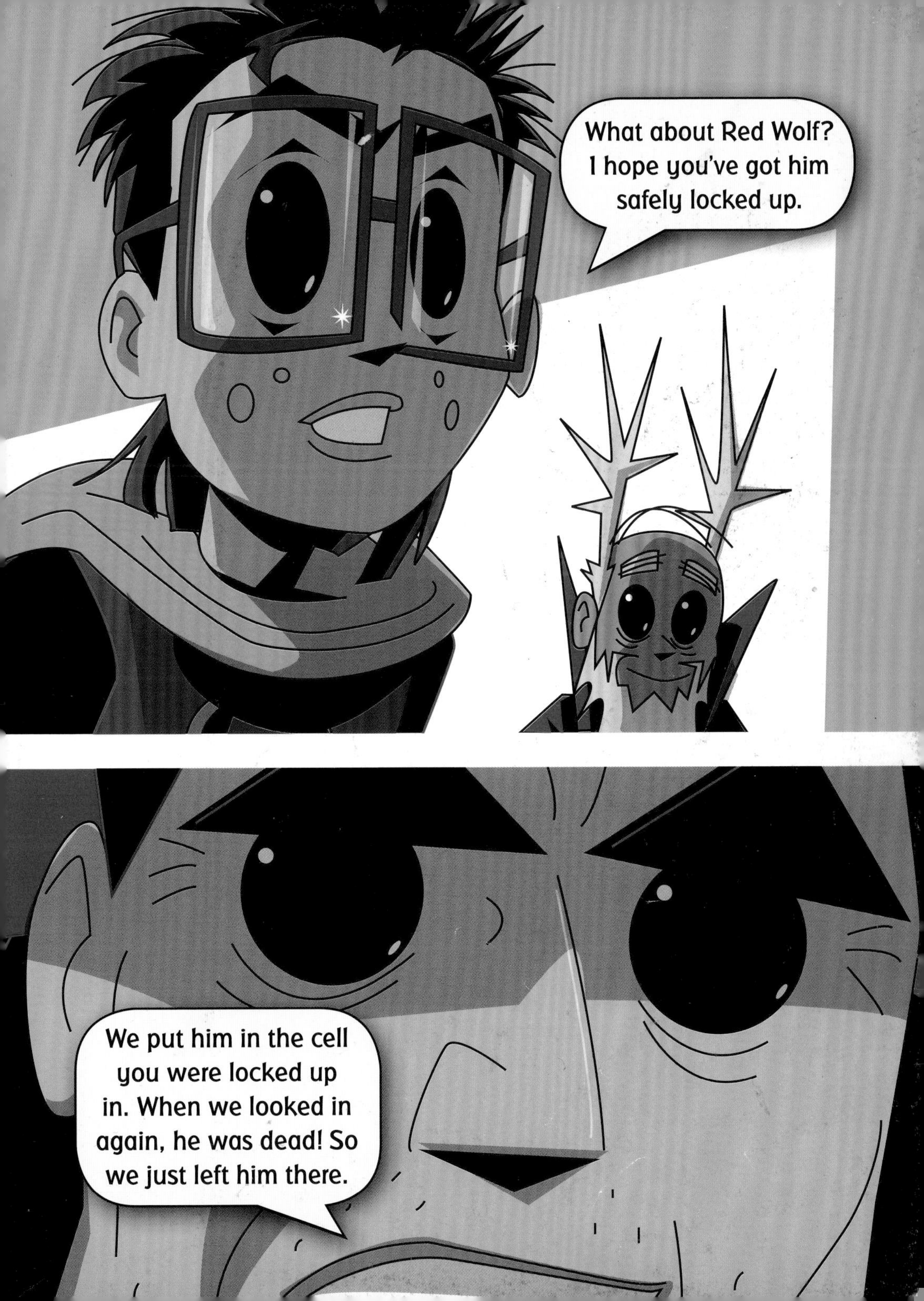
What about Red Wolf? I hope you've got him safely locked up.
We put him in the cell you were locked up in. When we looked in again, he was dead! So we just left him there.

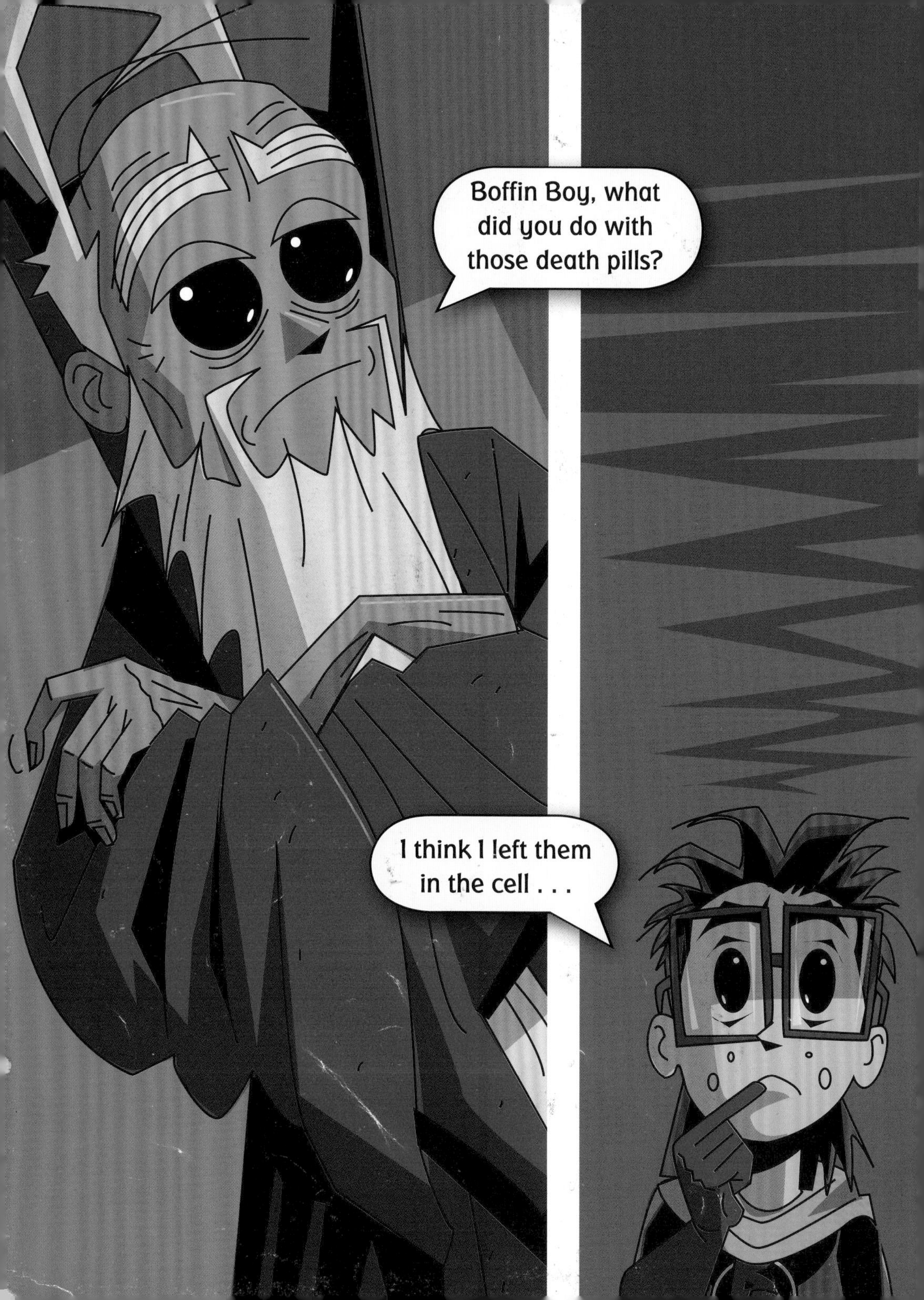
Boffin Boy, what did you do with those death pills?
I think I left them in the cell . . .

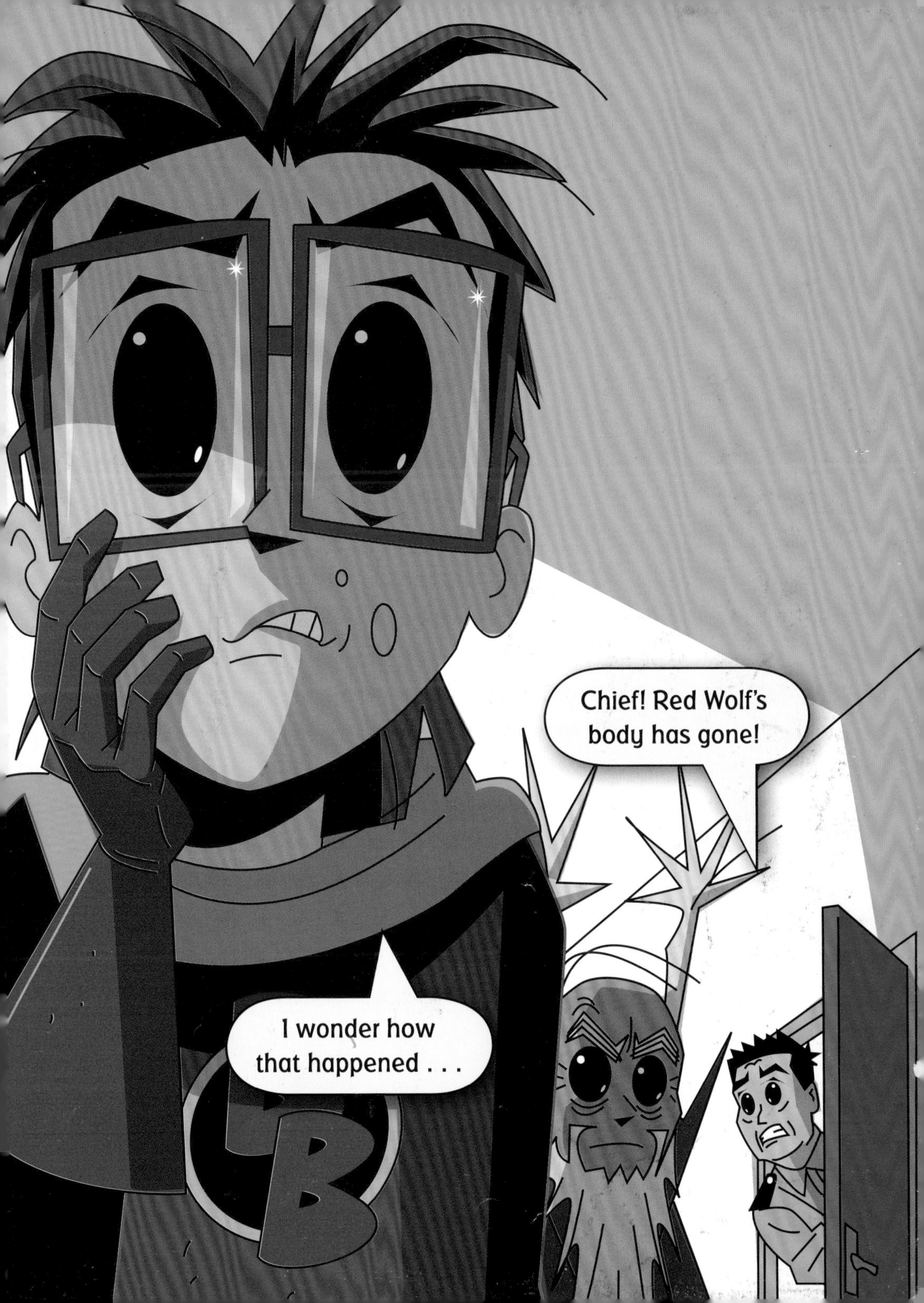
Chief! Red Wolf's body has gone!
I wonder how that happened . . .

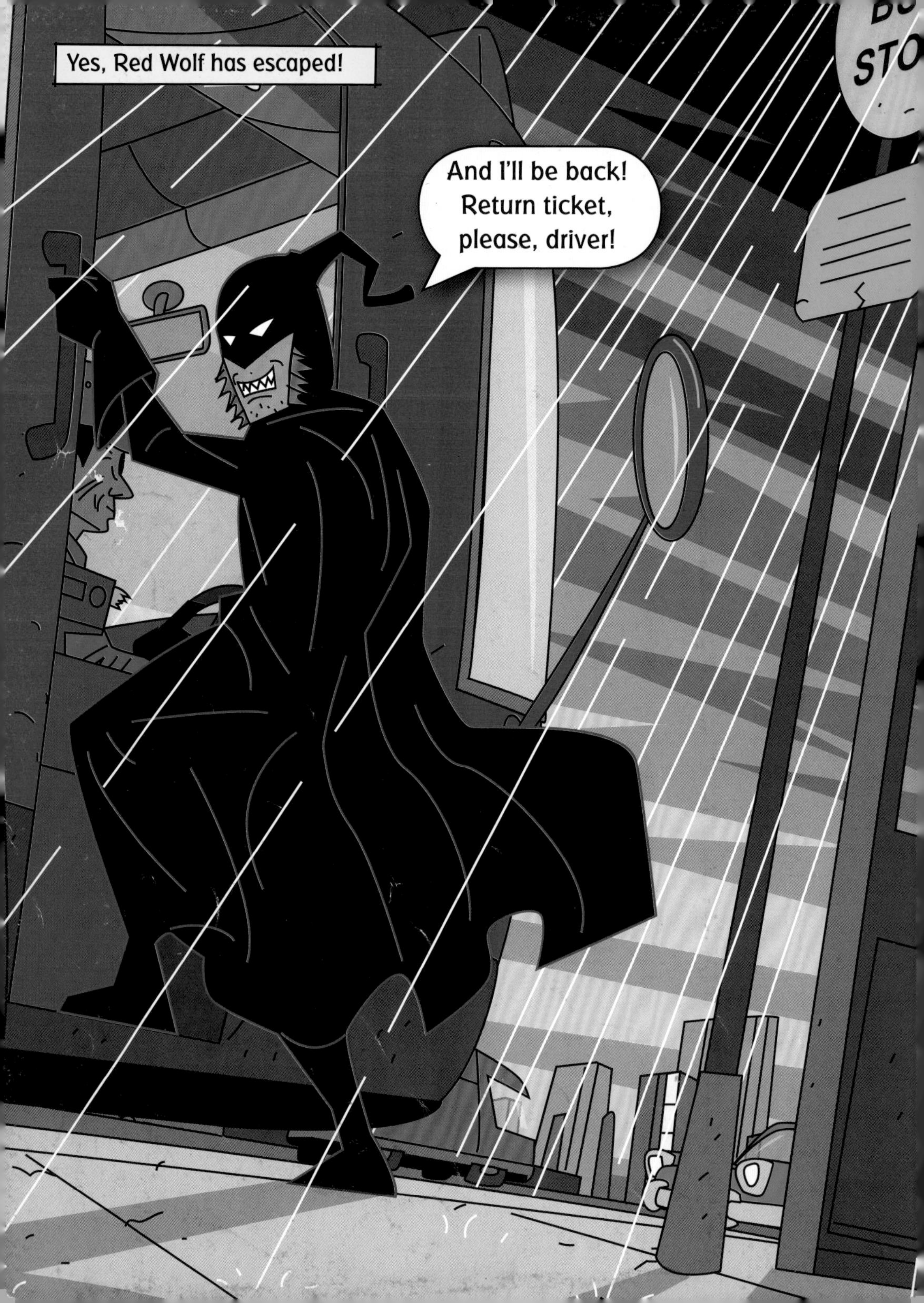
Yes, Red Wolf has escaped!
And I'll be back! Return ticket, please, driver!
BUS STOP

ABOUT THE AUTHOR

David Orme has written over 200 books including poetry collections, fiction and non-fiction, and school text books. When he is not writing books he travels around the UK, giving performances, running writing workshops and courses.

Find out more at:
www.magic-nation.com.

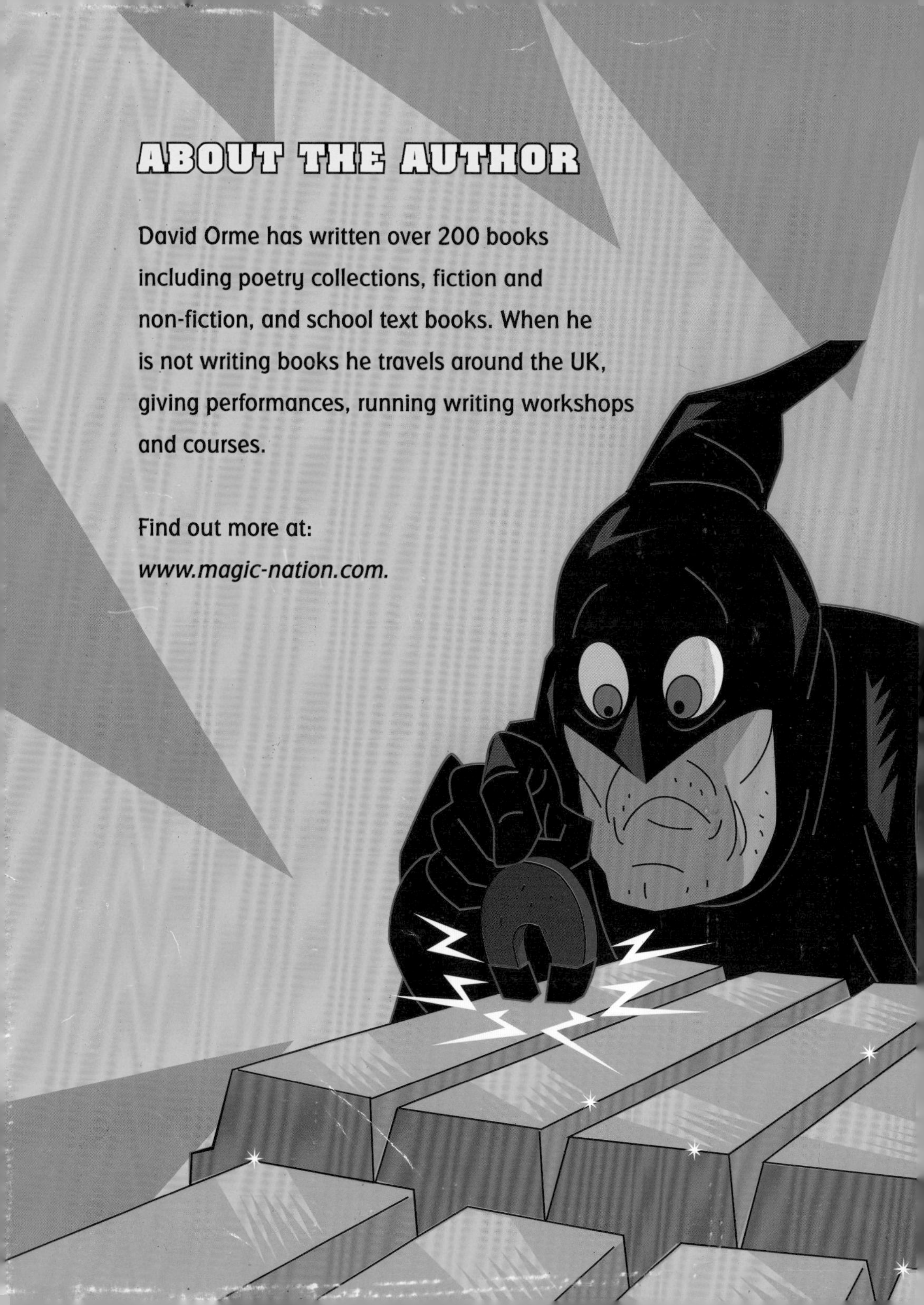